SNOW GLOBE

GEORGIA BEERS

SNOW GLOBE

THIS TRADE PAPERBACK ORIGINAL IS PUBLISHED BY BRISK PRESS, BRIELLE NEW JERSEY. 08730

EDITED BY KELLY MOLINA
COVER DESIGN AND LAYOUT BY STEFF OBKIRCHNER

FIRST PRINTING: DECEMBER 2013

ISBN-13: 978-0-98998951-0

By Georgia Beers

Novels

Finding Home
Mine
Fresh Tracks
Too Close to Touch
Thy Neighbor's Wife
Turning the Page
Starting From Scratch
96 Hours
Slices of Life
Snow Globe

Anthologies

Outsiders

Georgia Beers
www.georgiabeers.com

Acknowledgements

They say writing is a very solitary career, and that's true to an extent. But behind every solitary writer is a team of people who help get the final product into the hands of the reader. That being said, I'd like to thank my team.

Stefanie Obkirchner – thank you for your brains, your creativity, your nitpicks, and your friendship. You mean the world to me. When are you moving in?

Susan Meagher and Carolyn Norman – working with Brisk Press is easy and stress-free because of you two. Thank you so much for all you do to help bring my work to my readers. I hope you know how much I appreciate your efforts.

Kelly Molina – I hope we get to work together many more times in the future. Your editing was insightful yet gentle, positive yet thorough, and you made me feel confident about what I do. There are not enough words in the world to thank you for that.

My friends (both writer and non), my family, and my readers – you keep me going when I want to pack it in. Rachel and Melissa saw the first chapter of this book and helped me get it on track. Steff and Lynda helped me keep it there. My readers pushed me along with their notes of encouragement, and I am eternally grateful to all of you. You build me up with your letters and e-mails, your phone calls and messages. I wouldn't have the career I have if it weren't for your support. Thank you from the bottom of my heart. As always, I'll keep writing if you keep reading.

And last but never, ever least, my wife Bonnie. You are as responsible for this amazing career of mine as I am. I can't wait to sit at another bar with you, drinks in hand, and hammer out the next story. You are my rock, you are the wind in my sails, you are my partner in everything, and I love you for it. Heart.

Dedication

To each and every one of us who still believes in the magic of Christmas.

Chapter One

"KENZ. YOU CAN'T STAY in there forever."

Can't I? I glance at the small Pottery Barn clock on the shelf above the sink, do some quick math, and realize I've been sitting in my downstairs bathroom for nearly three hours. What's the rest of my life? Besides a complete train wreck?

Allison knocks some more. "Kenzie. Come on. You're better than this."

I snort loudly, making sure she can hear me. "I am? Really? According to who?"

"Whom."

I make a face, the same face I always make when Allison corrects me. "According to *whom*?" I amend, giving sarcastic emphasis where it is due. "Certainly not according to Kim."

"That bitch," Allison says at the same time I do, which—I have to admit—makes me almost smile. "What the hell does she know?"

"She knew she didn't want to marry me," I say, quieter now as the reality of my situation settles over me once again.

"We've been through this a dozen times," Allison says, trying to hide the annoyance in her voice, but failing only because I know her so well. "She's obviously an idiot, A. And B, look on the bright side. At least she jumped ship *before* the wedding and not after. Think of all the paperwork. All the wedding gifts you'd have to give back. Or sell on eBay."

Again, the faint ghost of a smile touches my lips. When I catch myself, I revert back to my pained scowl. No, there is no smiling. I've been dumped by my fiancée a mere nine days before our wedding. Who does that? Who that isn't in a romantic comedy on the big screen, I mean. Who? I glance up from my place on the linoleum floor, my back against the locked door, and my gaze falls on the small window. Snow is falling, gentle and soft, like the perfect Christmas postcard. That's what our wedding was supposed to be: the perfect Christmas postcard. We were going to be a regular Norman Rockwell painting, Kim and me. Our colors were burgundy and ivory, classy and festive. The décor for the reception hall was all pine boughs, candles, and sparkling ornaments, miniature white lights adorning every possible surface. I'd worked my ass off making everything just right. Most little girls dream of a June wedding. I've always wanted a Christmas wedding. It's my favorite time of year. The warmth, the celebration, the extra love and kindness that seems to ooze into every person throughout the month of December...I wanted all of that on my most special day. It was going to be so perfect, it felt almost too good to be true.

Of course, that's exactly what it ended up being.

Kim and I had been struggling as of late, that was true. But like a moron, I assumed it was simply wedding stress. *It happens to everybody*, I kept telling myself. *She'll be fine once everything is set*, I reminded myself daily. Except I was wrong, and I blamed myself for not seeing the signs. When I look back from my seat on the bathroom floor, they are all so clear. I picked everything. *Everything*. Colors. Food. Decorations. Minister. Invitations. Locations. Cake. *Everything*. Kim simply nodded and agreed to whatever I wanted. And I thought that was fine, perfectly acceptable, no alarm bells at all clanging obnoxiously in my head. My girlfriend was just that awesome. She wanted me to have the wedding of my dreams, so she let me make all the decisions. It had nothing at all to do with the fact that she was having second thoughts. Nothing. At all.

She left me by text.

Can you believe that? Who does that?

I pick up my phone and scroll to it for about the three hundred thousandth time in the past three hours.

I can't do this. I'm sorry. I don't want 2 get married. I'm still in love with Tina & I need 2 explore that, figure out what it is. I have 2 get out of here, out of town. I'm sorry. Ur a wonderful woman, & u deserve better. I'll have my stuff picked up from the house when I get back. Take care of urself.

That came this morning. December 11. Nine days before our wedding.

No phone call. God forbid, no actual face-to-face conversation. I've always suspected that texting would end up being the downfall of the entirety of mankind, but after this morning, I am sure of it. I remember watching *Sex and the City* years ago, and there was an episode where Carrie's boyfriend broke up with her by Post-It. I am certain Kim has taken things to a new low with her Text Dump.

So she was going to "have her stuff picked up," was she? I consider myself a mature woman. I'm thirty-five, not fifteen, but I admit the idea of completely trashing Kim's stuff crosses my mind, and as I sit on the hard linoleum, destructive scenarios zip through my head in quick succession. Toss her clothes out the window? Burn them in a sacrificial pile on the front lawn? Scribble in all her books? Snap all her favorite CDs and DVDs in two, then put them back in the cases so she won't realize they are all useless until she attempts to watch or listen to one? (This one is still a distinct possibility.)

"Mackenzie Ann Campbell." Allison's suddenly stern voice pulls me back to the present, and reality slaps me once again. "This is ridiculous. Come out here. Now."

"I'm staying in here forever."

"You can't."

"Why not?"

"You'll starve."

I hadn't thought of that angle. Hmm. "I have water." I look around in desperation, my eyes landing on the vanity counter. "And Colgate."

"Good idea. Maybe you can drop those last five pounds you've been complaining about for the past month. And you'll become famous as the inventor of the Toothpaste Diet. I like it. Good plan."

I grin. I can't help it. It's important to have a best friend who can always make you laugh.

"You're smiling," she accuses. "Admit it."

"I admit it."

"Good. Will you come out now?"

I sigh. Heavily. With great volume. "I don't know."

"Don't make me pull out the big guns, Kenz. You know I will." I don't respond, and she continues. "Okay. Fine. Just remember: you brought this on yourself." I hear her slide down her side of the door, and I know we are now sitting back to back. I find comfort in it, even though I know she is about to win this argument. She begins. "Two blondes are standing on a river bank, one on each side. The first blonde shouts across the water to the other, 'Hey! How do you get to the other side?' The second blonde looks to her right down the river, then looks to her left. She shrugs and shouts back, 'You *are* on the other side!'"

I snort. I can't help it. "Oh, that was awful."

Allison ignores me and continues. "What do you call a dead blonde in a closet?" I know better than to respond. She'll tell me the answer anyway as part of the torture. "The 1998 Hide and Seek Champion."

Laughter bubbles up out of me. "Oh my god."

"Why can't a blonde dial 911?"

I wait for it.

"She can't find the eleven."

"Okay, okay," I say loudly and stand up. "I give. You win. Just stop. Please." I unlock the bathroom door, open it, and look down at Allison, sitting on the floor and looking rather pleased with herself.

"Hi," she says.

I try to smile, but it feels like a grimace. She stands up and opens her arms. I walk into her embrace, and she wraps me up tightly, places a kiss on top of my head. The emotion I thought I'd beaten—at least for a while—comes back in a rush, and my eyes fill instantly. A quiet sob escapes me, and I feel Allison's arms squeeze me to her.

"Shh," she whispers. "It's okay. Everything's going to be okay."

I let her hold me for a while, allowing myself to fall apart one more time before becoming annoyed with all of it yet again. I pull back, sniff hard, wipe my eyes with the backs of my hands. "This sucks," I spit angrily. "This fucking sucks. I hate her."

"That bitch," we say at the same time, and we toss each other half-grins. Allison slides her hand down my arm and grasps my hand. "Come on. I'm getting you far away from that room." She leads me to the living room that I'd shared with Kim for the past eighteen months, the living room that is now mine alone, and sits me on the chocolate brown leather couch. "Sit right here," she commands. "Do not move." She punctuates this statement with her *I'm not kidding* eyebrow arch, then heads to the kitchen.

I sit obediently while she rummages around in my kitchen. Dishes clatter, the microwave beeps. I find a spot on the taupe carpet and stare at it so as not to look around the room at all the things that were once *ours* and are now *mine*. Scrubbing Kim from this townhouse will be a big undertaking, and right now, I don't even want to think about it. Except that's exactly what I'm thinking about when Allison returns to the room. She's carrying a huge plate of nachos smothered with cheese, black olives, and jalapenos. She holds up a finger, silently telling me to wait, then goes back to the kitchen. She returns with two Heinekens and hands me one.

"You're allowed to have two of these and that's all," she tells me as she holds my bottle slightly out of reach. "It took me almost three hours to get you out of that bathroom. I have no intention of being stuck back in there with you, holding your hair while you puke up a six pack and cry some more over your bitch of an ex." Her wink softens the whole thing, and she hands me my beer. Crossing the room, she grabs a DVD that I can't see and pops it into the player.

Allison Cieslinski has been my best friend for what feels like a hundred years, but in actuality is only about four. We met through friends at a party and just hit it off. I was fresh out of a relationship at the time. She had been in hers with Marianne for about two years. I did very little mingling at that party because I stood chatting with Allison and Mare all the while, joking and generally having a terrific time. It's Allison's sense of humor that draws people to her, that and her confidence. I've never met anybody as comfortable in her own skin as Allison. Her styles change. Her hair color changes. Her makeup techniques change.

She's always trying new things. Unlike me who, when I find something that works for me, tends to stick to it like glue no matter what—and no matter what year. Today, Allison's wearing one of what she calls her Dyke Outfits: low-slung jeans, a white T-shirt, and a plaid button-down shirt over it with the cuffs rolled up to her forearms. Kim used to take offense to that label, but Allison would simply say, "Why? I *am* a dyke, and today I feel like dressing like one. What's the problem?" Kim would just make a face and look away. Allison's hair is very dark right now (which is only slightly darker than her natural color), and she got it cut kind of short last month, so it doesn't quite reach her shoulders. I didn't expect to like the shorter cut as much as I do, mostly because Allison has the most awesome hair of anybody I know—soft and thick and just a little wavy—and I love it long, but this new style is really cute on her. Of course, now that it's short, she's working on growing it back out. As long as she doesn't dye it blue again. Two years ago. The one and only time I did *not* love her hair. But that's Allison. Always changing her look.

Remote in hand, she plops down on the couch next to me, grabs a chip and crunches it, then hits play. I know in about three point five seconds that she's put in *Aliens* for me.

"Nothing makes everything better quite like Sigourney Weaver kicking some ass," she reminds me, draping an arm across my shoulders.

I nod in utter agreement. "It's simply a fact of life. And just for today," I add, "alien, thy name is Kim."

Chapter Two

BEING LEFT SUCKS. IT is no fun. Frankly, I think it shouldn't be allowed, which is silly, I know, but that's how I'm feeling on Day Three. Six days from today, I was supposed to be walking down the aisle on my father's arm, heading towards the happiest moment of my life. But that's not going to happen. At this point, I don't know what *will* happen. Six days seems like forever from now. What will I be doing? Staring off into space? Plotting Kim's violent death? Hanging from my own shower rod? I don't know.

What I do know is that I won't be walking down the aisle into wedded bliss.

My phone rings, hauling me out of my own self-pity—which is probably a good thing. I glance at the screen of my cell and see that it's my mother calling. Probably not a good thing. I answer anyway because I am a good girl like that.

"Hi, Mom."

"Hi there, sweetheart. How are you today?" She's injected false cheerfulness into her voice, and it irks me.

"I'm fine, Mom."

Apparently, I'm a little snippy, because she answers with, "Look, honey, I know you're hurting, but if you don't want me to come over there so much, you need to at least let me call and check up on you and not be annoyed at me when I do it."

I suppose she's right. She was popping in every couple of hours over the past few days, and I finally had to tell her to back off. If I want to lie around in the middle of my living room floor surrounded by snot-filled tissues and wail about how horrible my life is while cutting Kim's face out of every picture in the house, I should be allowed to. Without my mother walking in and giving me a look of pity. I guess letting her check up on me via telephone instead of unannounced visit is something I'll have to allow.

"I know, Mom. You're right. I'm sorry."

"What are you up to today?"

I look around at the living room carpet littered with snot-filled tissues interspersed with bits and pieces of photograph scraps, most of which are Kim's face. "Um, not much."

"Are you going to work next week?"

That's a good question. Today is Saturday, and technically, I'm supposed to work for three more days next week. Monday through Wednesday, I work. Then I took Thursday off for last-minute things. Friday was going to be my wedding day. Next Saturday, Kim and I were scheduled to head off to this huge gay resort in Florida over Christmas. "I don't know," I answer honestly. My boss is pretty awesome. I am a technical writer and proofreader for a large manufacturing facility, and I can do a lot of my work from anywhere, so I'm sure if I call her and tell her my situation, she'd be fine with me taking some extra time to work from home. Of course, that would mean I'd have to call her and tell her my situation, and I do not relish that. Who wants to tell people they've been dumped mere days before their wedding? A wedding that person was invited to.

"Maybe it would be good for you if you worked," my mom suggests, as gently as she can. "Keep your mind off of things."

"Maybe." I sit up. My head swims, since a quick glance at the clock tells me I've been lying prone on the floor for two hours.

"I took care of the guests," Mom says, even gentler. "I called everybody."

I swallow, my eyes welling, more from embarrassment than sadness this time. "Thanks, Mom," I manage to croak out, trying not to picture the faces of family and friends as they absorb the news that I was ditched. I'm not sure which is worse, the expressions of surprise or those of pity that I picture in my head.

"It'll get better, honey. I promise." My mother can be pushy and overbearing, but she knows me, and she loves me, and when I'm in pain, so is she.

"Thanks," I say again.

"I'll call you later."

We hang up, and it takes all the strength I have not to flop back down onto the carpet to wallow some more. Instead, I focus on sitting upright. *How much of my time and energy am I going to let this mess take from me?* I suddenly think. And I am surprised by the thought, which I'm guessing is a good thing because maybe it means I'm making the slightest, teeniest, tiniest bit of progress. I mean, really, I can sit around for weeks, months, years even, and wonder what I could have done differently. Trusted Kim less? Not poured my whole heart into my relationship with her? Waited longer than a year and a half to decide to get married? The bottom line is, she's still in love with her ex. Isn't that something I maybe should have noticed? Fuck, yes. But I was in love with *her*, and when you're in love, so many important things get blurry and soft and fall out of focus.

I shake my head and stand up. Yes, I actually stand up. I feel like I've spent the majority of the past three days flat on my back. And not in a good way. My head swims again as I'm hit with a full-blown head rush, and I realize I haven't eaten more than a few bites of nachos with Allison since Wednesday night. I carry my stress in my stomach, so when I'm stressed out the first thing that falls by the wayside is my appetite.

My phone dings as I head into the kitchen, indicating I have a text. It's from Allison.

What are you doing?

I type back, *Standing in my kitchen.*

Eat a banana.

Sure enough, there is a fresh bunch of bananas on the counter that she must have left during her last visit.

Yes, ma'am, I type back.

That's what I like to hear. Dinner tonight?

I take a moment to think about it. My emotions are so swirly right now. I'm fine one minute, a blubbering mess the next. Such is the life of the dumpee, I suppose.

I may not be the best company, I text, being honest.

You don't scare me.

I smile. Everybody should have an Allison. *Okay.*

Just as I'm texting her that I haven't been to the grocery store in over a week, her text beats me. *I'll bring food.*

You know me so well. It's the truth.

Lucky for you. ☺, she texts back. Also the truth.

Allison goes back to work, I assume, since her texts cease. She spent a lot of time here yesterday, so she's probably working a Saturday to make up for it. She's a web designer and works from home, but she has much more discipline than I do when telecommuting. That little text exchange was probably what she considered her "break," and now she's gone back to whatever project she's working on. Don't get me wrong, I do my work when I work from home, but that doesn't mean I don't also do laundry, run to the store, and wander around Facebook as well. What can I say? I'm easily distracted.

I need to deal with my boss. I know this, but I can't imagine actually talking to her. I'm such a wimp. I blame Kim. I've always been a pretty strong person, but she's made me suddenly jumpy and worse, ashamed. If my mother took care of all the guests, then my boss already knows what happened and probably won't be surprised to hear my request. I take a deep breath and…text instead of call. Because I'm a coward.

Her reply comes immediately, which surprises me as it's a weekend. *Take all the time you need. Not expecting you back until after the 1st.*

That's a relief. I think. I squint at the screen. Not expecting me back until after the first? Why? Because I took time off for my honeymoon? Or because she thinks I'll need that much time to recover? I'm torn between being thankful and being insulted. I toss my cell onto the kitchen counter, grab a banana, and head upstairs to the second bedroom that Kim and I use—sorry, *used*—for an office. It has a desk and computer, but also a futon that we open for overnight guests. It's open now, flat, and has an unzipped suitcase on it, half-filled with summer clothes. My suitcase. There's a big empty space next to it where Kim's suitcase was, but she took that with her Wednesday morning after I left for work and she decided she was leaving for…somewhere other than here. I came up here to check my work e-mail, but instead, I stand in the middle of the room and stare at my suitcase.

Shorts. Tank tops. A few nicer outfits for fancy honeymoon dinners. A brand new bathing suit—the first two-piece I've had in more than ten years. I've worked hard on this body over the past eight months, cutting out as much processed food as I could, weightlifting, running on the treadmill (which I despise with every fiber of my being). I'm in better shape than I've ever been and now I have no occasion to wear my new bathing suit. I pick it up, hold it out in front of me. It's black. Sleek. It's got silver piping along the seams. It covers enough, leaves something to the imagination. When I tried it on in the store, I had visions of Kim untying the top with her teeth, wanting me so badly she could hardly wait. Now… With a sigh, I toss it back into the suitcase.

I should probably unpack what I've got in there, but I just can't summon the energy right now. Instead, I turn to the desk and sit, fiddling with the mouse to call up my e-mail. There are a few things there for me. Not too much, as people at work know I'm expected to leave by the middle of next week. My brain then decides to take a detour and think about all the people at work who know me, know I was about to get married, and now know that I'm *not* going to get married. I am probably water cooler fodder, and the thought turns my stomach, and I suddenly wish Kim was standing next to me right now so I could punch her in the face.

A couple things have been sent to me for proofing, but due dates for each of them are mid-January. People are starting to slow down, rush jobs are being turned away. It's the holiday season. Nobody wants to work. People want to relax, shop, spend time with their families. Our townhouse has no Christmas decorations up. At the time, it made sense not to drag them down from the attic storage area. After all, we weren't going to be here for the holiday, and we were so preoccupied with all the wedding stuff, it didn't make any sense to take an entire weekend (yes, I take that long to decorate…call me crazy, but I love it) out of our planning and organizing to arrange decorations we wouldn't even see.

Now, though, I miss them terribly. The snow is still falling outside. There is a Tupperware container on my kitchen table filled with my mother's Christmas cut-out cookies. And yet there is no tree in my living room. There are no lights surrounding my outside entryway. There are no stockings dangling over my gas fireplace. My house is Christmas-less, and it makes me even sadder than I already was.

When my eyes well up—YET AGAIN—I get angry and swipe at them roughly. Blinking the tears away to clear my focus, I see the e-mail list again and notice one from The Rainbow's Edge. I click it open, and it turns out to be exactly what I expect: the confirmation of our reservation to their resort from December 21 through December 28. I heave a huge, worn-out breath.

The Rainbow's Edge is fairly new. It's an enormous gay resort on a beach in western Florida, actually marketed as a giant gay cruise ship on land. It holds a maximum of three thousand guests when completely booked, and it's open to both gay men and lesbians. It's only been open for three years, but Kim and I have friends who've gone and did nothing but rave about it for over a month after their return. With more and more states legalizing same-sex marriage, it's become almost a gay wedding Mecca, complete with an entire floor of Honeymoon Suites.

Kim and I have one booked for a week.

I now realize that we *still* have one booked for a week.

Yet another goddamned wrinkle I will have to deal with, I think, and a fresh wave of hatred for my ex of three days washes over me. I was so looking forward to going there, to getting away from the cold and the slush and the dangerous driving conditions and the dry skin, all results of winter in the Northeast. I was so looking forward to lying on the beach and baking myself in the warmth of the sun and reading three or four books at my leisure and having cocktails with umbrellas in them at ten o'clock in the morning if I wanted to, just because I could. Because I was on vacation. Because I was on my Honeymoon. Because I'd just gotten married. God damn her for taking yet one more thing away from me this week.

I have the phone to my ear waiting for an answer, fully intending to cancel my reservations (and probably pay a hefty fee for doing so) when it hits me. Like a Mack truck, it hits me, and

14

the gentleman on the other end of the call—who says his name is Trent—has to ask if he can help me two and a half times before I find my voice.

"Yes, hi. Sorry about that." I clear my throat. "I have a reservation for next Saturday, December 21. My name is Mackenzie Campbell."

I hear computer keys clicking, and then Trent says cheerfully, "Yes, Ms. Campbell. You have a Honeymoon Suite booked for the week. Good thing. We're almost filled to capacity."

My confusion over whether I'm really going to do this dissipates as I say to Trent, "Can you tell me, is it possible to extend my reservation?"

"You want to stay longer?"

"Actually, no. I want to come sooner."

His voice broadcasts his surprise. "Well, that's unusual. Let me see..." More keys clicking. "When would you like to come, Ms. Campbell?"

"I was thinking of this Wednesday. The eighteenth." I was going to have to fight with the airlines to change my ticket, but I am prepared to do so. This feels too right not to.

"You're in luck," Trent tells me, and my smile grows wide. "I can put you in the same room three days sooner." I am giddy as I tell him to go ahead and put the extra three days on the same credit card he's already got on file, which is Kim's. "We'll see you next week, Ms. Campbell," he says as he signs off.

Now for the harder part.

I send a quick e-mail to Allison because I know she won't answer a text right now, but she'll know immediately that she's got an e-mail.

I'm going to call you in three minutes. Please answer. It's important.

I wait an actual three minutes before dialing. She picks up on the first ring, which I knew she would.

"Hey, what's up?" she asks.

"Why don't Polish women use a vibrator?" I ask in greeting.

"I give. Why?"

"It chips their teeth."

Allison snorts a laugh. "Funny. You called me in the middle of my work day to tell me a Polak joke?"

"It's been a while."

"That's true."

"But no, that's not why I called." I wet my lips and take a deep breath. "How is your schedule?" I actually already know the answer to this. Things get slow around the holidays for Allison, and she likes it that way. Nobody needs anything designed that can't wait until after the first of the year, when everybody starts fresh.

"It's pretty light," she tells me. "I've got a few things that I held so I'd have stuff to work on, but that's about it."

"Nothing pressing?"

"At this time of year? No. Not really."

"Good. How about a vacation?" I picture her squinting, her dark eyebrows meeting at the point just above the bridge of her nose.

"What do you mean?"

"Come to The Rainbow's Edge with me." I drop it quick, then let it sit.

"Come—" She starts, then stops, and I know she's thinking about it. I jump in.

"I need to get the hell out of here, Allie. The last thing I want to do is sit around here on the day I'm supposed to be getting married. You know what I'd rather do? Sit on a beach in the sun and get completely shit-faced on Mai-Tais. Maybe meet some new

16

people. Or not. Who cares? I just need to get the hell out of here, and I'd rather not go alone." I hear her breathing. I know she's thinking about it just as surely as if I could actually hear the wheels in her brain turning. I throw in the kicker. "It's already paid for. And I will buy your plane ticket."

"When are we talking?" Got her.

"Wednesday. That would give you almost three days to get your ducks in a row with work."

"Let me make a few calls."

Chapter Three

ALLISON WAS NEVER AFRAID of flying before 9/11. And she'd still tell you she's not afraid, that afraid is the wrong word. She just doesn't like it now. It makes her nervous. Her palms get clammy. Her head starts to pound. Every mechanical sound the airplane gives off makes her wonder what it is and whether or not it's normal. She's not afraid we'll crash. She doesn't worry we'll be hijacked by terrorists. Explanation eludes her, and she's a little bit embarrassed about it, even with me, because it's obviously something psychological. Her doctor gave her an emergency prescription for Xanax—just four pills at a time—and she's to take one an hour before she is scheduled to get on a flight. Which she did, washed down with a Bloody Mary at an airport bar.

We're in the air now, me next to the window, Allison in the middle with her head back, her eyes closed, her earbuds in, and her fingers gripping the armrests like the seat may eject her at any moment. I grin at her profile, then turn to gaze out my window at the earth far, far below.

I can't believe we're actually doing this. I mean, it's no less than I deserve for the stress Kim has put me through, right? Why not take the vacation? I'm the one who found the place, who suggested it. I did all the research. I booked the reservation. And if anybody needs to get away, isn't it me? I watch the white expanse below us get smaller and smaller as we continue to climb, and I realize, not for the first time, this will be my first and only Christmas away from home. No snow. No Mom and Dad. No family. No Christmas tree or stockings. It's a bit surreal, and for just a second, I feel a pang in my chest that feels like homesickness. It makes me wonder if I'm doing the right thing. I think back to the phone call I made to my mother telling her what I had planned. She didn't argue. She didn't lament how awful it would be to not have her whole family together at Christmas time.

There was no guilt trip at all. *At all.*

I feel a tiny smile tug up the corners of my mouth when I realize how *unheard of* it is for my mother not to freak out over not having all of her kids together for a holiday. By not showing one iota of hurt or disappointment—and I know how hard that must have been for her—my mother made it clear to me that I am doing what I need to do, and that she understands it. I send up a little telepathic thanks to her. Or…send it down. Whatever.

Before I can stop myself, I wonder what Kim is doing. Right now. Where is she? Is there any guilt whatsoever about ripping out my heart and stomping on it? Is she thinking about me at all or is all her focus on Tina? And when my mind turns to Tina, I immediately—yet again—start pummeling myself for my oblivious stupidity. How exactly does one not notice that one's girlfriend is still in love with her ex? Just exactly how blind does one have to be to have a detail like that float right over one's head? I sigh and let my head drop back against the headrest.

"Stop it."

I look to Allison. She hasn't moved. Her eyes are still closed. She still holds the armrest in a death grip. "Stop what?" I ask.

"Stop beating yourself up."

My eyes widen. "How do you *do* that?"

She opens one startlingly blue eye, trains it on me. "You're not that complex, Kenz."

I give her a mock glare and stick out my tongue as she returns to her previous position. Then I chuckle, if for no other reason than she's right.

❄

We touch down in Florida right on time, and the change in the weather from home to here is so drastic, it makes me stop walking for a second and just stand there in shock. We left twenty-seven degrees and snowing; we landed in eighty degrees and sunny. For a split second, my brain feels completely scrambled.

Allison hooks my arm and drags me along with her so the people I'm blocking will stop giving me dirty looks. We follow the signs to Baggage Claim, grab our stuff, and look for the shuttle to the hotel. Allison spots it first.

"There it is." She starts walking toward it.

"It's pink," I say, unnecessarily.

"Of course it is."

And it's not just pink. It's *pink*. Like, hot pink. With flamingos, palm trees, and scantily clad men and women holding various tropical umbrella drinks painted all over it. Very subtle.

We hop aboard and sit among three women and four men, all smiling and all pinging my gaydar in a big way. The air conditioning is blasting in the shuttle, but I take off my hooded sweatshirt anyway. It's been almost three months since I wore something short sleeved, and despite my ridiculously pale skin, I relish sitting there in just a T-shirt. I relax and watch as palm trees and convertibles zip past the windows, the entire tableau almost foreign to a girl who grew up in the northeast. There is a little grass, but what I see is different, the blades wider, almost like a sawgrass of some sort. No snow, obviously, but also few hills. It's very flat and very dry. The majority of the trees are palm trees, and while I think palm trees are very cool, it's December and the utter lack of anything evergreen is a bit weird to me. To give credit to the Floridians, though, I see no less than a dozen Santa hat-wearing flamingos as we drive, so there's that.

"How you all doing?" the shuttle driver asks us over the intercom system, the sudden loud voice scaring the bejesus out of me. I think he got us all because of the slightly uncomfortable chuckle that runs through us like a small wave. He's a cheerful African-American man with shoulders the size of a small mountain. Like the flamingos, he is sporting a Santa hat.

"Great!" one of the male passengers enthusiastically answers. "I am so ready to par-tay!" He's small—probably an inch or two shorter than my 5'6", but in fantastic shape, all broad shoulders and flat tummy. I can tell because his lime green T-shirt fits him like a second skin. Before I can automatically relegate him to the box in my head marked "Self-Absorbed Gay Man," I realize that if I had abs like his, I'd wear shirts that were two sizes too small as well. I shrug with acceptance.

Two of the women are sitting very close together, holding hands and sending occasional loving glances at one another. They have the stink of newlyweds wafting off them, and I wrinkle my nose and look away. Right into Allison's eyes which are glittering in amusement. She arches one brow, and it's as much of a gentle accusation as if she'd actually said something. I stick my tongue out at her yet again, annoyed that she knows me so well.

"There it is," one of the male passengers says excitedly.

I turn to look out the window and am stunned.

I knew The Rainbow's Edge was big. All the advertising says so. There are five wings that hold over a thousand rooms of varying size and style. It boasts eight restaurants, six bars, three fitness centers, four pools, and five night clubs. The entire top floor is all Honeymoon Suites. Now, as I take in the actual building itself, I'm struck speechless. It's enormous. *Enormous.* The entrance where our driver pulls to a stop is dead center and wings spread out in both directions like tentacles that go on forever. The architecture itself is a bit of a mix of traditional Greek and current Florida, ivory in color with gold and copper molding, trim, and fixtures on windows and doors. The realization that Kim could still have come and it's totally realistic that we'd never run into one another—let alone be able to find each other—makes me almost bark a laugh out loud.

Employees seemingly appear from nowhere to unload our bags, and their uniforms actually match the building itself...and each other. For some strange reason, I flash on the Oompa Loompas from *Charlie and the Chocolate Factory* as they scramble to take care of all of us. Allison is faster than I am, grabs our stuff, and slips our driver a tip. I know better than to argue with her because it'll be like this the whole trip (unless I beat her to the punch). She's already informed me that since she's staying for free and I paid for her plane ticket, she's getting everything else that she can.

I take that as a challenge.

To say the lobby is opulent would be a gross understatement. Marble floor. Fancy gold trim. Seriously. It's almost laughable in its ornateness. It totally would be if it wasn't also sort of beautiful. There's a fine line between classy and overdone and The Rainbow's Edge walks it nicely. The huge fountain of gold and ivory stands in the middle and shoots a stream of water into the air a good fifteen feet at least and is circled by various men and women sitting on the edge, some conversing, some looking at phones, some people-watching. Off to the right is a large and open double-doorway where darkness lays beyond and a pumping bass beat oozes out. One of the clubs or bars, I'm sure.

Allison gives me the head bob toward the registration desk, and I walk over to check us in, happily surprised to see Trent ready to take care of me. He is exactly as I pictured him on the phone: tall, thin, and gorgeous with twinkling green eyes and waves upon waves of dark hair. His bronzed skin would send Kim Kardashian scrambling to the nearest tanning salon in a panic. I smile and give him my name, which he recognizes.

"Ah, Ms. Campbell." He leans forward and gives me a wink. "Or should I say Mrs. Campbell?"

I open my mouth to explain and correct, but ultimately decide to leave it alone. Telling a complete stranger about my relationship woes and how I am actually on my honeymoon with my best friend instead of my wife is not the way I want to begin my vacation. Even if I am about to check in to the Honeymoon Suite. I give him a grin instead and nod like I've been immersed in marital bliss for the past week rather than wallowing in my own grief and self-pity.

"You and your lovely bride are in Honeymoon Suite two-zero-zero-six on the twentieth floor. I think you'll be very happy with the amenities, and we've left you a little something to start your celebrating off on the right foot." He hands me two key cards wrapped in a classy little envelope that's ivory with gold print, and I'm once again struck by how very matchy-matchy everything is. "Enjoy your stay, and please let us know if there's anything we can do to make your time here better."

I thank him and return to Allison, who is standing with our bags like a lone island in a sea of homosexuals as they flow around her. Men and women alike are moving through the lobby in various states of happiness and joy. Everybody's smiling. Couples are holding hands. Five women spill out of the bar across the lobby laughing and joking, obviously just this side of intoxicated. And for a small moment in time, I am happy to be here, despite the crappy circumstances that brought me.

"Ready?" I ask Allison.

"This place is incredible," she tells me, as if I hadn't noticed, watching the quintet as they pass us.

"I can honestly say that so far, it's lived up to the hype." We spend a moment watching the fountain. "Ready?"

"Lead the way."

We roll our bags to a bank of elevators, and grab one that's open. Inside, are the five women from the bar. I push the twenty, noting that the ten is also lit.

"Hi," one of them says to Allison as her friends try to stifle giggles. She's got short blonde hair, spiked up in the front. Her face is very tan and her eyes are pale blue. Her Bermuda shorts and polo shirt label her "golfer" in my head within five seconds. She points to the black leather bracelet that encircles Allison's slim wrist. "That's really cool."

"Thanks." Allison gives a half-grin and fingers the bracelet, a Christmas gift from me last year.

"And that dimple in your chin?" She leans in close and almost falls into Allison. "Sexy."

"Don't mind her," a ponytailed redhead says, trying to hold her friend upright. "She's drunk."

"*You're* drunk," Spikey Blonde replies, pushing at Pony Tail. With seven of us in the elevator, there's not a lot of room for Pony Tail to stumble to. The tall woman behind her holds her up as Pony Tail looks at me with raised eyebrows that say, *See?*

The elevator dings at the tenth floor and empties out most of its cargo, Spikey Blonde shouting, "You're cute!" on her way down the hall. The doors slide shut completely before Allison and I burst out laughing.

"Is that a preview of our stay?" Allison asks me, still laughing. "If so, it's going to be a hell of a vacation."

"I'm trying to decide if I want my goal during my stay to be to end up just like that or to avoid ending up like that. I'm really not sure."

We get off on the twentieth floor. The hallway is so long, it reminds me of the scene in the movie *Poltergeist* where JoBeth Williams is trying to get to her kids' room and the hall just gets longer and longer as she stands there.

"Wow," Allison comments. I nod. What else is there to say?

We follow the hall to our room, I slip in the key card, and we enter. And both stand there in awe.

"Wow," Allison says again. Again, I nod because there is nothing else to say.

The room is huge and it's situated on a corner, so there are windows on two sides. Huge windows. Floor-to-ceiling windows. The curtains have been pulled all the way back, but the sheers have been left as covering. I walk over and pull them aside, and I gasp at the stunning view. Palm trees, sand, and miles upon miles of water out one set of windows, complete with a small balcony. The city itself out the other. It's breath-taking, and I suspect at night, it'll be even more so.

The bed is beyond king-size, is round, and has what seems like two dozen pillows on it, all in variations of burgundy, ivory, and gold. It's not lost on me the irony of the room being the same colors I chose for my wedding, but I work hard to let it go.

The counter on the far wall has a Keurig coffee machine with an abundant selection of flavors, plus a box containing a sophisticated mix of teas. Next to that sits a shiny silver ice bucket filled to the brim with fresh ice cubes and a bottle of what looks to be decent champagne from where I stand. Two flutes are rims-down next to it, along with a glass plate of chocolate-dipped strawberries and a tented sign that says simply, Congratulations in an elegant script. I look away from it, and my gaze lands on the Jacuzzi tub tucked into the corner near the Travertine tile bathroom.

Allison kicks off her shoes and pads across the plush burgundy carpet to the tub. "Oh, we are so filling this up while we're here. More than once." She actually climbs into it and sits down. It's deep. I can only see her from the neck up. "Nice," she says.

I'm still standing in the middle of the room, and it's weird because I'm not really sure how to feel. It's a gorgeous room. Stunningly gorgeous, and I'm proud of myself for picking such a fantastic place for my honeymoon. But I'm not on my honeymoon, and that's something I think I'm still absorbing.

I don't notice Allison getting out of the tub, but suddenly she's behind me and has wrapped her arms around my middle. She sets her chin on my shoulder, and when she talks, I can feel her breath in my ear.

"It's okay, Mackenzie," she says, her voice quiet. "You're going to be fine. We're going to have a great time here, just you and me, and we're going to make sure of it." Coming around in front of me, she grabs my hands, and her face lights up in a wide smile. "I mean, come *on*. Look at this place!" She drops my hands and spreads her arms out wide like a circus ringleader. "How can we not have a fabulous time here?" Turning to the counter, she pulls the bottle from the ice bucket. "First things first." The cork makes a festive pop as she releases it from the bottle and then pours. She hands me a flute, and I'm struck—not for the first time—with the silly thought that champagne is actually rather pretty with its sparkling bubbles.

Allison leads me to the edge of the bed and we both sit. Raising her glass, she says, "To my best friend, Mackenzie. Thank you for bringing me here with you. And to Kim—that bitch," we say that part together, "you are forever the stupidest woman on the planet." I can't help but laugh.

We clink and sip and the champagne is *very* good.

"I admit," Allison says after a moment, "I was a little worried about sleeping arrangements, but we won't be able to find each other in this bed if we tried."

I laugh in surprise because it hadn't even occurred to me that there would only be one bed. "Right? It's like the size of a football field."

"And that view."

"I can't wait to see it after sunset. Hey, maybe we'll be able to actually see the sunset."

"That would be cool."

We're silent for a while, sipping our champagne and watching the ocean, which I realize is actually the Gulf of Mexico. I mentally shrug, knowing I'll probably still refer to it as 'the ocean.'

"What should we do now?" I ask her.

"Isn't it obvious?" She waggles her eyebrows. "We go to work on those strawberries."

Chapter Four

STUDYING A MAP OF the entire hotel is not easy, if only because the place is *mammoth*. If it was a shopping mall, it would be Kim's idea of Hell with the endless wings and winding corridors, not to mention the fact that we need a map to find anything. She despises shopping and not being able to find her way around—let alone find her way *out*—would send her right over the edge.

The visual of that pleases me for a quick second.

We've decided to hit the pool as soon as we settle in. Well, Allison has decided to hit the pool. I've decided to hit the bar at the pool. Yes, I am aware that getting totally shit-faced is probably not the best way to spend my un-honeymoon, but at the moment, it feels like a good idea.

There are four drawers in the cherry wood dresser, so I take the top two and Allison takes the others, and we unpack. The counter in the bathroom has, conveniently, two sinks sunk into the granite top, so we each claim one and unload our toiletries. I have about three times as much stuff as Allison, but she simply smirks and doesn't bust on me for it. For now.

We take turns using the bathroom to change into pool attire. That's a funny thing about lesbians who are friends, isn't it? We don't like to change clothes in front of each other. Doesn't matter that we're not dating or not interested or whatever. We just feel like it's...I don't know, inappropriate? Allison exits the bathroom with board shorts and a light T-shirt over her bathing suit. I pop in and change as well, but have decided against wearing the bikini. Allison notices immediately when I come back into the room.

"No suit?"

I shrug. "Nah."

"How come?"

I glance at her, and those eyes harbor nothing but kindness and concern. I've never been able to lie to Allison. I'm not sure how she does it, but she makes it impossible. I flop onto the bed.

"I just don't feel…sexy," I say, trying to explain. "I need confidence to pull off wearing a bikini. And I feel like I had it and Kim took it away from me."

"That bitch," Allison and I say simultaneously. She grins.

I try to smile, but I can feel it falter on my lips. "What did the blonde say when she saw a box of Cheerios?" Allison asks.

I shake my head, adoring her for trying to keep me from wallowing. "I don't know."

"Oh my god, donut seeds!"

I throw a pillow at her.

Allison checks the map one more time—we've chosen the West End Pool, which seems to be closest to our wing—as I put sun screen into my bag, along with the map and my key card, and we head out.

"Can you put my iPod in your purse, too?" Allison asks me as we wait for the elevator.

"I don't have a purse."

She raises a dark eyebrow and looks pointedly at my bag.

"It's a bag," I inform her.

"It's a purse."

"I am a lesbian. I don't carry a purse. I carry a bag."

"Really?" She waits. I wait longer. She finally huffs out a breath. "Fine. Can you put my iPod in your *bag*?"

I take it from her with a flourish. "Of course. I'd be happy to."

The West End Pool is big and blue and swarming with guests. Some are in the water, others are lounging on chairs. Even more are wandering, obviously scoping. Music is pumping over the speakers, some of the house music you hear at the gay bar at home, all throbbing bass and unintelligible lyrics. Christmas lights are strung everywhere, and all the bartenders and employees are wearing Santa hats. We snag two towels from a rack on the way by. Allison immediately commandeers two lounge chairs for us, but I tell her I want to sit at the bar under the awning for a bit. She nods, knowing all about how easily I burn. She does not have my bad luck. She tans a deep bronze. I don't recall ever seeing her with even a hint of sunburn in all the time I've known her.

I leave Allison her iPod, find a stool at the bar with surprisingly little difficulty, order myself a rum runner, and have a beer sent to her. When she gets it, she holds it up toward me, and we silently cheer from twenty feet apart. The drink is not as weak as I expected it to be at an all-inclusive resort.

It's interesting to watch a large space occupied by both gay men and lesbians. We're so utterly different in personality and presentation, and I take some time to just observe. Most of the men are in Speedo-type suits, tanned, lean, and doing their best to show themselves off to the other gay men there. There are also others…a few bears over in the corner wearing trunks, one slathering sunscreen on the hairy back of another. A smattering of older gay men can be seen if I look for them, most in more discreet bathing suits and sunglasses, some with thinning hair or even sun hats. You can tell they're watching the younger, sleeker men. Frankly, so am I. Some of those boys are stunningly gorgeous.

The lesbians are a different story, and not for the first time, I find our community so interesting. A large percentage of us are overweight. I'm not being facetious; I'm stating a fact. I like to think it's because women are less critical of their partners when it comes to physical appearance, but I don't know for sure if that's it. I am one of only about a half dozen women with hair long enough to put in a ponytail. The overwhelming majority of the women here have short haircuts. I see four bikinis. The rest of the swimsuits are either one-piece—and most of those are racer-backs —or a combination of board shorts and swim shirts. The more athletic and boyish of the women seem to favor the shorts/shirt combination. They also seem to be in their twenties. While most of the men are frolicking in the water or strolling along the edge of the pool, most of the women are in chairs and reading or listening to music, as Allison is doing when my traveling gaze gets all the way around the pool and stops on her.

She's wearing a black one-piece suit and looks nothing short of elegant. She has made lying on a chair in the sun and bopping her head gently to the music coming from her earbuds seem completely effortless. Yet again, I wonder how she does it, how she just exudes such confidence, such comfort with herself. As I'm rolling that around in my head, I notice a small group of young dykes standing in the pool, talking and gesturing subtly—or so they seem to think—in Allison's direction. They laugh collectively, and one of them hops out of the pool to the encouragement of the others. She's cute. Lanky, athletic, with short brown hair and a row of silver hoops traveling the edge of one ear. She gives herself a shake, apparently hoping to garner some confidence of her own, and begins to walk.

I sip my drink and say out loud, quietly, "And three...two... one..."

"Hi there."

The voice next to me startles me so much that I actually flinch. I turn away from Allison and face the source of the voice. She's

31

maybe forty, forty-five, with short brown hair. Sunglasses are perched atop her head and when she smiles, crow's feet appear at the corners of eyes nearly the color of rust. The tiny lines are not unattractive. In fact, they make her seem wise. She's wearing an emerald green bathing suit with a sheer white cover-up over it.

She gestures to my drink with her eyes. "Can I get you another?"

I am about to refuse, which is my automatic reaction after being in a relationship for nearly two years, but I stop myself. This being single thing is going to take time to get used to. "That would be great. Thank you."

We both know the drink isn't costing her anything, but the act of actually ordering it for me seems…chivalrous in a way, and I like it.

"Sandy," she says to me after ordering two rum runners, and holds out her hand.

"Mackenzie," I respond, and we shake. Her hand is warm, smooth.

"Come here often?" she asks, then grins.

"Not once," I say.

On the other side of me, the athletic woman in shorts and shirt is ordering two beers, one of which is Allison's brand. I quickly glance her way, and she catches my eye and winks.

"She yours?" Sandy asks, nodding in Allison's direction.

I follow her gaze. "Her? No. Oh, no. She's my friend. We're here together. Well, not *together*, together. Just together. As friends. As in friends together." I want to stop and drop my head into my hands, but I manage a weak smile instead and try to otherwise occupy my mouth by sipping my drink. The athletic woman leaves with the beers and sits down on what's supposed to be my lounge chair, hands a bottle to Allison.

"Where are you from?" Sandy asks, lassoing my attention back to her. I detect a very slight drawl.

"Oh. Um, New York."

"I *love* New York. I need to go back. It's been too long. Last time I was there, I saw *Rent* on Broadway."

"Yeah, I live in upstate New York."

"Ah. I see. Can you take the train into the city?"

I sigh. Why do people always think if you're from New York, you mean New York City? There is a huge state aside from the five boroughs, but out-of-staters seem to rarely notice. "Well, I could take the train into the city," I tell her. "But it takes about eight hours. I live *upstate*, upstate. Like, I'm on the border of Lake Ontario. I'm practically Canadian."

"Oh," she says. "Oh! I get it. So, nowhere near New York City."

"Not terribly close, no. But my part of the state is gorgeous. We have a lot up there. Lakes and wineries and beautiful state parks. It's really something." I realize as I'm saying it that it's exactly how I feel. I love my hometown. I love my home state. I feel even more strongly about that being in a state that's completely flat, hot, brown, and has bugs the size of my dinner plates.

"So you must have left some snow behind, huh?"

"I did. Not a ton. A couple inches. We usually get hit hard come January, though." I sip my drink. "What about you? Where are you from?"

"North Carolina. Raleigh."

"I love it there," I say. "My brother went to NC State. I visited him a few times."

"I went there too. Small world."

I lift my glass. "To small worlds." We cheer.

We talk for quite a long time, drinking and chatting. Sandy is fresh out of a relationship, too, and her friends dragged her to The Rainbow's Edge to take her mind off the upcoming holiday. We share our stories, and I am honest about mine—I wasn't sure I would be until the whole thing tumbled out of my mouth before I could stop myself. She nods, is properly sympathetic, and I detect...something in her demeanor. The slightest change? An infinitesimal pulling back? I'm not sure, but it's like the air between us shifted just a tad.

We talk a bit longer. I say I'm here until after Christmas. She's leaving the day before. Our drinks finished, she slides off the stool.

"Well, Mackenzie, it's been very nice chatting with you." She holds out her hand for another shake, which I oblige her.

"Same here," I say. "Thanks for the drinks," I add with a wink.

"Any time." And she's on her way.

I watch as she leaves, wondering what, if anything, just happened. Was it something I said? Am I paranoid?

I grab another drink for myself—making a mental note that this needs to be my last one for a while—order a beer, and head over to the lounge chair next to Allison. Athletic Cutie is gone, frolicking in the water with her pals again. Allison removes her ear buds and takes her beer from me.

"You let her down easy?" I ask Allison, gesturing with my eyes.

"Please," she says with a snort. "She's, like, fifteen."

I laugh. "She is not."

"Okay, twenty-five. Maybe."

"You say that like you're fifty."

"Some days, I feel like it." In truth, Allison is thirty-seven, and I can see how somebody twelve years her junior might be a hard sell. Still, I have many friends who are coupled with partners many, many years their junior. Or senior.

34

"She was cute," I say, meaning it.

"Agreed." We're silent for a moment, then Allison says, "What about you? What happened to the professor?"

I furrow my brows. "Who?"

"The one you've been chatting with. Didn't you think she looked like a professor?"

With a chuckle, I realize she's right. "She did, didn't she? That was Sandy. Yeah, she was nice."

Allison is looking at my face intently. I hate it when she does that. It's like she can see all my thoughts, and it kind of unnerves me. "What's the matter?"

I shrug. "After I told her about Kim, she sort of...pulled back. Is that not something I should share?" I'm asking honestly because I really don't know. I'm not a liar, have never been good at it. "I mean, I'm not here to find a new partner." I say this with a scoff, like that's the most ridiculous thing I've ever heard. I may be overselling it, though it's the truth. I'm too battered and beaten by Kim. I am so not ready for somebody new. But does that mean I shouldn't even talk to anybody? Shouldn't be interested? Shouldn't *show* interest?

Allison makes weird movements with her lips to indicate she's thinking. "I guess maybe I'd wait for the second conversation for that." She rolls her head on the lounge so she's facing me, and flips her sunglasses up so I can see her eyes. "You can say you're recently single, but maybe wait on the 'I was practically left at the altar' part for a later discussion. You know?"

I nod. It makes sense. Allison's pretty wise about this stuff. Still, I don't like that there's a stigma around me now. I didn't think about it at the time, but Allison's words cleared it up. Sandy probably left wondering what kind of crazy person I must be for my fiancée to leave me less than two weeks before we were to be married. I blow out a breath. *Thanks, Kim.*

Chapter Five

THE RAINBOW'S EDGE HAS a plethora of options for food. There's casual dining, sports bar dining, fancy-schmancy dining, and everything in between. Because we just got here and we're still getting the lay of the land, Allison and I opt for casual dining this evening. Also because neither one of us feels like dressing up.

Allison's wearing a cool pair of khaki colored cargo shorts, a black V-neck T-shirt, and some cool Merrell sandals that I decide immediately I will borrow in the very near future. Like, on this trip. She throws on a little makeup and some silver jewelry, and the outfit goes from plain to classy. I shake my head in envy, as I've never been able to make dressing seem that effortless.

"You suck, by the way," I toss over my shoulder as I head to the bathroom.

"Um, thanks?"

I stress a little bit over my outfit, and it frustrates me because that wasn't something I'd planned on. I thought I'd be here with my new wife, and the only person I was worried about impressing was her. Now, again, I'm blindsided by the fact that I'm single, and I suddenly find myself concerned about whether or not I'll be attractive to other women. With a loud groan, I pull on a pair of black capris.

"Stop it," Allison says through the door. "You're beautiful, and you don't have to impress anybody."

I pull on a pale blue short-sleeve top and exit the bathroom. Allison gives me a once-over. "You're not wearing *that*, are you?" she asks.

My entire face falls, I can feel it.

Laughter busts out of Allison. "I'm kidding," she says, earning a punch in the arm from me. "You look fantastic. Hurry up. I'm starving."

I throw on some mascara and a little lip gloss, and we're off.

Allison has obviously been studying the resort map because she's got the layout down pat already and leads us to the restaurant without any hesitation.

"Impressive," I tell her as we're shown to a table for two.

She shrugs, but the little tilting up of the corner of her mouth tells me she's glad I noticed.

The restaurant has a predictable nautical setting, but it's tastefully done, and I find myself having fun looking at the various sea-faring items on the walls and such. Enormous anchors, boat bumpers, an occasional life preserver. A piano and its player are tucked into a corner, a tinkly-sweet version of *I'm Coming Out* drifting through the restaurant.

"Really, when do we get a new theme song?" I ask Allison as we peruse the menus.

"Let's hope he doesn't launch into the Muzak version of *It's Raining Men*," she replies.

Our waitress is adorable. I won't lie. She's a tiny little thing with a blonde ponytail and a diamond stud in her nose. Her smile is contagious, her skin, flawless, a sprinkling of freckles dotting her rosy cheeks. Also, I have apparently become invisible because she only has eyes for Allison.

"Hi there. What can I get y'all to drink?" she drawls, a gentle southern accent the icing on the cake.

Allison smiles and says, "I'm going to have a Blue Moon, please."

"You got it."

"And I'll have a dirty martini," I say. The waitress nods and jots down my drink, but doesn't look at me. She rattles off the specials, to Allison, then leaves with a promise to be right back with our drinks.

"Wow," I say.

"Right? She's cute."

I snort. "She is, but my hair could be on fire, and I don't think she'd notice."

Allison looks confused.

"Pay attention when she comes back."

We return to the menus, and I'm thinking since I'm at a beachfront resort, I should eat as much seafood as I possibly can. Torn between the broiled scallops and the ahi tuna, I ask Allison about her choice. Of course, we both know she's getting a steak.

Our drinks arrive, we place our orders, and I am soundly ignored for the most part. The waitress heads off to place our orders, and Allison immediately busts out laughing.

"I told you," I say.

"Oh, my god. That was painfully obvious."

"I guess at an all-inclusive resort, you can afford to completely disregard half your customers without worrying it'll affect your tip." I hold my glass up. "Anyway. Screw her. Here's to my best friend, taking pity on an old, abandoned woman and going on vacation with her. You're the coolest."

"You're not old, and you're not abandoned," Allison says tenderly. "I am, however, the coolest. That part's true."

We clink glasses and sip. The first swallow of my martini goes down like lighter fluid, just as it should. I make a face (that usually helps it burn less) and look around the restaurant.

Obviously, I've been to gay bars before, other gay organizations where everybody there is gay, lesbian, bisexual, transgendered or somewhere in between, but I've never been someplace of this scope. This restaurant is as big as your average Olive Garden or Applebee's, but every person in here is like me. And not only that, the restaurant is a tiny fraction of this resort. There are seven other places to eat, and probably at least a couple of them are bigger than this one. Everybody in this entire resort is like me. Well, a large majority. I realize I don't know for sure if the employees are all gay —probably not—but still. I have never been someplace where the overwhelming majority of a pretty large population is just like me. It's a really cool feeling, and it goes a long way in alleviating my self-consciousness.

"I like it here," Allison says, interrupting my thoughts as if reading them.

"I want to go to Provincetown," I blurt, apparently taken with the idea of being surrounded by gay people.

"Now? Maybe we should finish this vacation first."

I grin. "No, not now. But I've never been there. I want to go."

"Okay. We'll go."

Our salads arrive, and for a micro-second, I entertain the idea of jumping up and down and waving my arms in front of the waitress's face just to get her to look at me. I think better of it.

The food is fabulous. I've never done an all-inclusive vacation before, and this one includes everything. We stay inside the gated area that encompasses the resort and everything is "free." Not souvenirs at the gift shop or that sort of thing, but all the food, all the drink, and the overall cost reflects that, believe me. This is not a cheap place to stay. That being said, I was surprised earlier by the quality of my drinks at the pool. I am equally impressed with my meal tonight. My tuna is wonderful, Allison's steak is cooked to perfection, and despite the horrific circumstances that brought me here, I'm happy I made the trip anyway. Screw Kim.

We take our time eating, talking easily like we've always done, or enjoying companionable silence, also like we've always done. It's one of the things I adore most about my friendship with Allison: we're so easy together. We can talk about anything. We don't have to talk about anything. Either way, we're perfectly comfortable. I've never had a friend like that before.

We split a slice of cherry cheesecake. I get the pointy end because Allison loves the crusty part. It works well. Before I can stop it, a yawn stretches out of me just as Allison asks a question.

"What's next? Want to check out a bar or two? Maybe go dancing?"

I don't love to dance. Allison is one of the few who can actually coax me onto a dance floor. I contemplate going with her, I do. But I feel like all the stress of the past few days, the packing, the flying, the newly single status, has tiptoed up behind me and just sat on my shoulders. I am utterly exhausted. I hate to let Allison down, but I just don't think I can do it tonight.

"I'm beat," I say. "Can I take a rain check? Tomorrow night?"

"Of course. Do you mind if I go?"

"Not at all. You don't have to stay with me every minute, you know." I catch her eye. "Not that I don't love spending time with you, but you're on vacation too. Please don't feel like you have to babysit me. I'll be fine."

Allison sets her fork down, folds her hands, and sets her chin on top of them. She blinks those blue eyes at me for a long moment before she says anything. "First of all, I do not feel like I have to babysit you. You're a big girl. You can take care of yourself. But I do want you to know that I'm here. If you need something— even if that something is for me to sit in the room with you and watch *NCIS* until my eyeballs bleed—I can do that. Just say the word. Okay?"

I nod, touched. When I can find my voice, I say simply, "Thanks, Allie."

"Hey, what are friends for?"

The cute little waitress—who I've now decided is more elflike than sexy—brings our check, and I sign off on it.

"That was awesome," Allison says as we stand.

"Absolutely. I'm torn between trying the other restaurants and just coming back to this one for the duration of the trip."

Allison grins and extends her arm, allowing me to exit ahead of her. Outside the restaurant, she turns to me. "You're sure you don't mind if I go exploring?"

"No. Absolutely. Go."

She studies me for a moment. "You're not going to slip into the land of Wallow and Cry, are you?"

I tip my head to one side, give her a look of slight annoyance. "No. I'm just going to crash."

"Promise?"

"I promise. You have your key?"

She holds hers up.

I wave her on. "Have fun. Be good. But not too good." I give her a wink.

"I'll be quiet when I come in." She gives me a quick kiss on the cheek and leaves me standing alone outside the restaurant. One corner of my mouth quirks up when I realize she knows exactly where she's headed. She's always been a whiz with directions. Me? I'd walk in circles around the same fountain sixteen times before I realized it.

With a sigh, I head for the bank of elevators that will take me back to my room.

It's interesting to feel so alone in a place so filled with people. I pass a gaggle of men who are happily perpetuating the gay male stereotype not only through their ridiculously coordinated outfits, but by giggling like children and calling each other "gurl!" I can't help but smile at them. Not far behind them is a quartet of women —two couples judging by the hand-holding. They nod and smile as they move past me. At the elevators, I wait with a dozen others, all smiling and happy, and for a moment I bitterly wonder where the lesbian drama is. There has to be some. You can't have this many lesbians in one place and not have drama. It just doesn't happen. Somebody's got to be checking out a woman other than her partner. There must be a lothario someplace putting the moves (or at least the eyes) on somebody else's woman. I cannot possibly be the only lesbian in this entire, gigantic resort who's heartbroken and lonely.

Can I?

I stand in the back of the elevator and listen to snippets of three different conversations going on around me. It's a big car, and I smile because I'm always quiet in an elevator and these people obviously have no such behavior. They babble on. One guy's criticizing the sandals of another (I like them; I'm not sure what Critical Guy's problem is). An older woman is raving about her meal, and I wonder if she ate where I did. A middle-aged woman is listening intently as the woman next to her lays out exactly how she should make her approach to the "hottie" she's been flirting with mercilessly for two days.

Little by little, everybody exits until I'm the only one left in the car to the twentieth floor. It's early—barely nine o'clock—and the hallway is silent as I pad along to my room. Inside, the lights are starting to come on outside, offering up a stunning view in an attempt to keep me from falling into the funk I know is imminent.

There's still half a bottle of champagne left in the ice bucket. The ice is gone, melted into water, but the water is still cool and the champagne still has bubbles. Good enough. I pour myself a large glass, contemplate a soak in the Jacuzzi, but instead drag a chair to the windows that look out over the ocean, and have a seat. For long moments, I sip and watch, sip and watch. I'd love to be able to keep my mind empty, but that's always been difficult for me. It's why I don't sleep well. If I wake up in the night, my brain starts churning out thoughts—about work, about family, about life, about things around the house that need to be done, about upcoming events—it's crazy and it's almost impossible to turn off once it gets started. So of course, as I sit here sipping champagne and trying to enjoy the lovely view, my mind decides we need to revisit my being on my honeymoon alone because my fiancée is in love with somebody else.

I suppose I should garner a tiny consolation from the fact that Kim didn't fall for another person while we were together. She's still in love with her ex. It's not a good thing. It's not a happy turn of events for me. But I guess it would have been a lot worse if she'd fallen in love with somebody other than me and it had been new instead of old.

I contemplate this as I polish off the glass of champagne and help myself to another.

Kim's face fills my head, and I sigh because I knew it was coming. Really, how could I expect to be here without her and not feel…shitty? Allison's presence helps, it's true, but it's not a cure. I can spend every waking hour for the next fifty years with Allison and that won't change my reality. The woman I love—loved—no, still love—I think—agreed to marry me, helped me plan a wedding (okay, 'helped' is a relative term here), waited until less than two weeks before said wedding, and then sent me a text telling me she's still in love with her ex. *That* is my reality. I can recite it over and over and it doesn't change.

What do I do about that?

Evaluate my feelings? That sounds so dumb, but maybe it would help. I have no idea. I do know that I'm angry. I'm hurt. No, hurt is too light a word. I'm crushed. I'm devastated. I never expected to be devastated, not at any point in my life. Who does? But she devastated me. Which brings me back to the anger. Hurt and anger together are a nasty combination, mostly because there's not a lot you can do to alleviate either. I could throw things. Break things. Sometimes that makes me feel better. Unfortunately, I'm someplace where none of the breakable things belong to me, so breaking them could end up being rather…costly, not to mention disrespectful. I glance at the thirty-seven pillows on the bed and think about hurling them around the room, but I'm not really able to picture any satisfaction coming from pillow tossing.

I swallow more champagne, then hold my glass up and study it.

I could get drunk. Why not? Drunk is good. Drunk helps you forget, at least for the moment.

There's enough champagne left for half a glass more. Not quite enough to get me good and drunk, but enough to get me a little beyond tipsy. I empty the bottle into my glass and enjoy the view for a bit longer. I can see a large ship way off in the distance, its light visible on the horizon. The palm trees sway in a gentle breeze coming off the water. People mill about along the beach under the lights. It's gorgeous. Stunningly gorgeous, and for one moment, I'm glad I'm here to absorb the view. In the next moment, my eyes well, and I'm sad that I'm sitting here alone, on my honeymoon alone, because the woman I loved didn't love me back.

When the room is completely dark, I stand, deposit my empty glass on the table next to the empty bottle, and flop onto the bed. I can still see out the window. With just my eyes, I follow the lone ship along the horizon until I can't make it out any longer. And I think of it as me, a lone ship sailing slowly through the night, quietly, unobtrusively. I absently wonder at its destination, thinking that if it's anything like me, it probably doesn't have one.

Chapter Six

MY HEAD POUNDS ONLY slightly, like a quiet drum rather than an obnoxiously loud marching band, when I open my eyes. The digital clock reads 10:47, and the room is bright with sunshine. I'm on my stomach, my arm above my head and under my pillow. At least I think that's where my arm is. I'm guessing because I can't feel it. At all. I pull it out, and it flops off the side of the bed like a dead tree branch, the tingles beginning almost immediately.

"Shit," I mutter and sit up. I'm trying to massage some feeling —and circulation—back into my limb when the bathroom door opens and Allison comes out in her bathing suit, shorts over the bottom. Her hair is wet and slicked back, and she smells like soap and shampoo. She's a very pleasant sight.

"Good morning, sunshine. How's the head?"

She grabs the sunscreen off the dresser and slathers it on her legs with her back to me. That's when I notice a few things. First, there is a row of pillows down the middle of the bed, like sand bags lining a bunker. Second, I am in a T-shirt and my panties, and I'm reasonably sure that's not the outfit I went to sleep in. When Allison turns back around, she's holding the empty champagne bottle, waggling it from side to side.

"I thought you promised me you wouldn't wallow."

"I didn't," I reply, sounding more like a six-year-old than I care to admit. "I just…didn't want the champagne to go to waste."

"Uh-huh." She continues to apply sunscreen. And to look at me. I look away, point to the pillow line-up.

"What's going on here?" I ask.

"Oh. Those are the chastity pillows."

I furrow my brow.

"Remember I told you I'm a big cuddler? I didn't want you to wake up and have me wrapped around you like an octopus. The chastity pillows will keep that from happening so I don't freak you out." She smiles. A hank of wet hair has fallen into her eyes.

I nod at her explanation, then pull at my T-shirt, look at her questioningly.

"Yeah." She sets the sunscreen down and heads to the bathroom, tossing over her shoulder, "I didn't think you'd be terribly comfortable sleeping in your capris, so I helped you put on some jammies." From inside the bathroom, she adds, "Getting you out of your clothes was easy, but getting that T-shirt over your head? What a giant pain in the ass. It was like dressing an oversize rag doll."

The blow dryer turns on, and any response I might have had is drowned out by the sound. Which is just as well because I have no response. I must have been drunker than I thought last night. I don't remember passing out, but does one ever remember such a thing? Worse, I have no recollection at all of Allison coming into the room, saying anything, and certainly not helping me undress.

I close my eyes, blow out a weary breath as embarrassment washes over me.

When Allison comes out of the bathroom, she takes one look at my face and stops in her tracks. Sitting next to me on the bed, she puts her hand on my shoulder and says simply, "Stop."

"Stop what?"

"Stop being embarrassed. It's no big deal."

I shake my head slowly from one side to the other. "I'm not this person, you know. I'm not this weak, fragile, marshmallow of a person. I'm strong. I mean, I'm usually strong." I look at my feet. "I thought I was strong."

Allison turns and folds one leg up on the bed so she's facing me. "Kenzie, listen to me." She waits until I'm looking at her before she continues. "You don't have to be sorry. You don't have to be embarrassed. I don't think you're weak, and you're certainly not a marshmallow. You've been my best friend for almost four years. Don't you think I *know* you?"

Her eyes are warm and kind, her expression open, and suddenly, I feel safer, and for a brief moment, I think curling up in her arms and staying there for the foreseeable future is a fabulous idea. Instead, I nod.

"Kim did something awful to you. That's a fact. How could you not be affected? Should you be polishing off bottles of champagne?" She gives me a raised-eyebrow look. "Probably not, but who can blame you? Another fact is that it's going to take you some time to bounce back. That's normal. But," she holds up a finger, "you *will* bounce back."

"You think so?"

"I know you, remember? You're a bounce-backer." She winks and stands up. "And you have me to help. Now get dressed. We're going to get you a good breakfast, and then we're going to catch some rays today. A nice, easy day by the pool. Put on your suit. I've got the sunscreen and the books. We're going to be vegetables today. Nothing but relaxation. Oh, and I booked you a massage later this afternoon. Sound good?"

"Sounds great," I say, because it does. I watch her tossing things into a tote bag. "Hey, Allison?"

"Hm?" She turns to look at me.

"Thanks."

Her smile is wide. Allison's got a great smile, and it emphasizes the little cleft in her chin. "Absolutely."

My energy renewed, I hit the bathroom.

We opt for the West End pool again, and it is as happy a place as it was yesterday, though it seems like more Christmas decorations were put up overnight. A couple of the potted palms have miniature white lights dripping from them. More lights are strung along and above the bar, as well as the refrigerators behind it. The bartender is incredibly sexy, dressed in cut-off denim shorts, a royal blue bikini top, and a Santa hat. Around her neck dangles one sleigh bell that she jingles when she gets a tip.

Allison and I grab a couple towels and choose a pair of lounges not far from where we were yesterday. It must still be a bit early for the pool crowd because while there are a couple dozen people here, it's not nearly as populated as when we were here yesterday. I let Allison take care of ordering our drinks, and when she returns, one sip of mine tells me it's straight orange juice. I shoot her a look, and she winks at me.

I don't mind, actually. I'm full from a delectable breakfast of fruit-stuffed crepes and about four cups of coffee, so I don't even really have the room for a cocktail. Probably a good thing. I spread out my towel, get comfortable, pull out my e-reader.

The weather is stunning, and for a moment, I just soak it in, let it absorb into my skin. Sunshine, electric blue sky, probably around eighty-five degrees. It's picture perfect, and if it weren't for the decorations and the sporadic playing of a holiday tune over the speakers, it would never occur to me that it's December 19. I haven't checked the weather at home, but I'm sure if it's not snowing, it will be. And there is something unsettling for a northeastern girl about being in beautiful, sunbathing weather less than a week before Christmas. Not to mention how alarmingly pale my skin is compared to the people who live here; it's easy to distinguish the visitors (most of us) from the natives (most of the employees and a few of the guests). I can hear my mother's voice in my head warning me about sunburn and melanoma and I set my e-reader down to slather on a bit more sunscreen, just to be safe. I'd like to have a deep, bronze tan. I'd like to not have skin cancer more. Plus, as I said before, I don't actually tan. I pink. Then I peel. Then I go back to white. It's sad, really, and so unfair.

Allison, already on her way to bronze, stretches out in the chair next to me.

"I could get used to this," she says.

"I know, right?"

"People are actually working today. Doesn't that suck?"

"For them. Yup."

I slide my sunglasses onto my face, which makes for better people watching, since it's not as obvious when I'm staring. Again, it's a nice mix of men and women, and I'm reminded of how often we do not do things together. It makes sense, I suppose. We're all considered homosexual, but really, what do we have in common? The gay men friends that I have love to do the things I hate: shop, throw theme parties, watch *What Not to Wear*. And I love to do the things they hate: play sports, camp, watch football. Okay, that's a lie. I don't really like to camp. In fact, I hate it. All the bugs, dirt, and gross bathrooms I have to share with other dirty people? No, thanks. But I keep that to myself mostly, because I hear they can kick you out of the Lesbians Club if they find out.

The other end of the pool seems to be the men's side, and I watch as a couple of ridiculously handsome ones sit on the edge with their feet dangling in the water. Behind them in two lounge chairs are two older men watching them, occasionally leaning into each other to say something quietly. I wonder if each of the older men are partnered with each of the younger ones. Or are the older ones together? Are the younger ones a couple? I squint, hoping if I just look hard enough I'll figure it out.

"The hottie on the left belongs to the older guy on the right," Allison says softly next to me.

"How do you know?" I ask.

"Because the older guy on the left has been checking him out since we sat down."

"Ah. I see."

"Hey, isn't that your bar buddy from yesterday? The professor?"

I follow Allison's gaze, and sure enough, I see Sandy and a couple other women heading toward the bar. She's definitely still cute, even though she dropped me like a hot potato last time we were together. I admire her long legs, her athletic form. She's got sunglasses on today, so I can't see her eyes, but as soon as she turns her head in my direction, I snap mine down and pretend to read. I'm subtle like that. I hear Allison snort next to me, and I reach across to slap at her.

I look up again too soon. Sandy is looking my way and gives me a little wave. I wave back, then return to my e-reader that I'm not reading. I'm trying to project indifference. I want her to know I don't care that she darted away like a scared rabbit yesterday, that it didn't sting. Why would it sting if I don't care?

This entire circle of thought annoys me, and I decide to read in earnest.

Best idea I've had in a while because the book turns out to be really good and two and a half hours fly by before I know it. Allison sets a cocktail on the table between us. I grab it and sip without looking, which pulls my gaze from my book as I realize it's a real cocktail.

Allison shrugs at me. "I figured it was time."

I give her a grateful smile.

"Your massage is in an hour," she reminds me.

I get myself to the end of a chapter, bookmark my spot, and flip the cover closed on the e-reader. Taking a few minutes to finish my drink, I look around. Things have really picked up since I stopped paying attention a couple hours ago. The crowd has doubled in size, at least, and I notice the same segregation as before. On the one hand, I find it a little sad when we share the same trait for which we've been discriminated against for centuries. At the same time, I don't really want to be any closer to Joe Coppertone and his yellow Speedo that isn't leaving a damn thing to the imagination, so segregation is fine by me. I shudder.

I grab quick directions from Allison as to where I'm going to take my clothes off for some random stranger and let him or her rub my body all over, make her promise to save my chair, and I head back to the room to rinse the sunscreen off. I make it to the massage suite with five minutes to spare.

The receptionist is a nice, handsome gentleman named Rob (and seriously, is every employee here gorgeous? Is that a prerequisite for getting hired?), and he leads me to a warm, comfortable room. The music is a quiet version of something possibly Native American given the primitive wooden wind instruments used, but it's relaxing. It's right when I'm thinking that I really like this entire room that I notice an awful smell. Patchouli. I feel myself grimace, then try to hide it as Rob turns to me with a white cap-revealing smile and tells me to take off however much of my clothing I am comfortable taking off, that Stella will be right with me.

No sooner does the door close behind Rob, then I am immediately on the hunt for the source of the dreaded patchouli. Why do people think that's an okay general scent for everybody?

It's horrid. It offends me. I'm actually on my hands and knees in frantic search mode when I finally find a Glade plug-in stuck in the outlet behind a chair, and I yank it out. I know I shouldn't, but it's a smell that I just can't stand. I know the room will still reek of it, but I can rest easy knowing there won't be any added patchouli stench, at least while I lay here.

Proud of myself, I toss the plug-in into a drawer. I disrobe down to my panties, slide under the blanket, face-down, and absently wonder how long it will be before anybody notices that the patchouli has wafted away to nothing. Uncontrollably, I giggle as I lay in the little head donut thing. Of course, that's the moment Stella walks in, and I quickly change the giggle to a cough.

"Hi, there. I'm Stella," she says, in that quiet voice that all massage therapists use. I guess it's so they don't startle you, but I immediately flash to an episode of *Friends* where Phoebe agrees to massage Monica. She uses the same breathy voice when she walks in that Stella is using on me. I wonder if she practices it at home. Of course, I then recall that Monica makes sex noises while getting a massage, which makes Phoebe massively uncomfortable. One of my favorite episodes. The giggle hits again before I can morph it into another cough.

"Everything okay?" Stella asks me, and I feel her hand on my calf.

"Fine," I say, pulling myself together. "I'm good."

I don't pull my head up to look at her, deciding to make it a fun game. I will invent her appearance. As she tells me what she's going to do (I've had massages many times, so I'm familiar and only pay slight attention), she walks near my head. She's not wearing any shoes, but has fun tan socks on with black paw prints all over them. I like Stella already. I like her even more when she pulls the blanket back and goes to work on my body, kneading my muscles into submission. I make a mental note to thank Allison even as I drift in and out of awareness. Stella's hands are strong, but gentle. Firm, but coaxing. It occurs to me that she'd most likely make an amazing lover with those hands. She hits a particularly sensitive spot on my right shoulder and I groan. Of course, groaning flashes me right back to *Friends* and I laugh.

"Did I tickle you?" Stella asks, stilling her touch.

"No. Not at all. I was just thinking…" I'm not sure if she'll be offended, but at this point, I'm feeling relaxed and happy, and I just want to be honest. "Did you ever watch *Friends*?"

"The one where Monica makes sex noises when Phoebe massages her?"

"Yes!" We're both laughing now. "I'm sorry. I just…my brain went there as soon as I made that sound."

Stella is still chuckling as she gets back to work. "It's okay. Happens all the time, actually. Sometimes *I'm* the one whose brain goes there. Imagine trying to explain that to your client. 'Oh, I'm sorry, sir, I was just thinking about you making sex noises while I massage you.'"

Our laughter dies down as she finishes with me. Half an hour is just not long enough for a massage, but it's better than no massage at all. Stella pulls the blanket back up to my shoulders, thanks me for my business, and tells me to take all the time I need to get myself dressed. I don't need much; I'm feeling surprisingly energized, rather than sluggish and wanting a nap as I usually feel after a good massage. On my way out, I am told that Allison has already paid for my time there. I leave a tip for Stella and see a sign for couple's massages. An idea hits, and I lean in to talk to Rob.

Chapter Seven

BACK IN MY ROOM, I stand in the shower to wash off the oil Stella used on my skin. It smells great, and I hate to lose that aspect of it, but it feels slick and greasy, and I need to get it off me. Under the hot spray of water, I bend my head forward and let the water beat on the back of my neck. I'm utterly relaxed, and if I didn't think I'd fall asleep immediately and possibly drown, I'd fill up the Jacuzzi tub and soak for a while. Maybe tonight.

It's weird, the way I feel. I gaze down at my toenails which are painted a deep purple and wonder at the convoluted trail mix of thoughts my brain has thrown at me since I arrived in Florida. There are times, like during my massage, like reading in the sun next to Allison, that I feel fine. I feel confident and content and *normal* and I don't miss Kim at all. Isn't that weird? And other times, like last night alone in my room, like all day tomorrow, I'm sure, I feel totally lost. Completely shattered and adrift. How can both sets of feelings—both opposite sets of feelings—exist in the same person in the space of twenty-four hours? Am I just going insane? Is that it? Have I lost my mind, and there is just no semblance of control in my psyche any longer?

The fact that I'm not devastated every second of every minute of every day has got to say something. Right? I'm hoping it means I'm making progress, but there's a small fraction of my brain that wonders if that's not a sign of something else. I shake my head, water flying around the shower, because I don't want to think about it. I don't want to think about what any of this might mean. About my former relationship. About me. I don't want to know. Not right now.

As I'm stepping out of the shower, I hear the door to the room open, and Allison calls hello to me through the bathroom door.

"How was the massage?" she asks.

"Not long enough. Wonderful, but not long enough."

"Female massage therapist?"

"Yep."

"Cute?"

I stop rubbing my arm with the towel as I realize I have no answer. "I have no idea. I never looked." I laugh. "She had cute socks on, though."

I can hear Allison chuckling. "You goof. How could you not look?"

"Her name was Stella," I offer lamely.

"Which tells me nothing about whether she was cute."

"Well, we'll have the chance to find out tomorrow because I'm going again, and you're coming with me." I wrap the towel around my body and exit the bathroom.

Allison is lounging on the bed, feet crossed at the ankles while she channel surfs. Her face is flushed from the sun, and a few reddish highlights are starting to make an appearance in her dark hair. She gives me a quick scan, which makes me smother a grin. "What do you mean?"

I scrape my bottom lip with my teeth, then tell her. "I booked us a couple's massage for tomorrow."

She raises her eyebrows. "Really?"

"Tomorrow is the big day," I remind her. "I'm afraid you may be stuck with me for the duration. I figured this was something you could enjoy along with me. I booked us for an hour."

Allison seems to ponder it, then gives me one nod. "Cool." She clicks off the TV, and levels her gaze at me. "As for tomorrow, I will be with you as much or as little as you want. Okay? If you need me every minute of the day to hold your hand, I can do that. If you want to be alone, I'm okay with that too. You just have to tell me. All right?"

I'm so touched by the sincerity of her words and her desire to take care of me that my eyes well, much to my embarrassment. "All right," I say softly. "Thanks."

We have dinner at a different restaurant than last night, though not before Allison feigns a plea to go back to last night's place to see if the waitress still has the hots for her. The food is as delicious as our previous dinner (I went with the haddock this time), but instead of heading back to the room again, Allison has convinced me to go dancing with her. As usual, I'm not sure how she managed it; I'm not a fan of dancing, and she knows this. I'm not very good at it (unless I've had several drinks), but she is, and she loves it. I figure after the sweet offer she made me about tomorrow, going dancing with her for a while is the least I can do to say thanks.

The club is dark, with purple neon and lots of black lights tucked into strategic areas. I can only tell where they are when Allison turns to talk to me and her teeth light up like glow-in-the-dark piano keys. The music is incredibly loud, the bass pounding so intensely I can feel it in the pit of my stomach. Allison leans close, her lips so close against my ear they send a shiver up my spine.

"What do you want to drink?"

I tell her Jack and Coke, and she makes a gesture that tells me to sit tight, so I lean against the wall to wait. She heads away from me toward the bar, her hips swaying to the music. I notice a handful of women check her out as she passes, and I grin. One woman taps the woman next to her, points, and they both watch Allison walk by. I can't blame them. Allison is hot; there's no doubt about it. I've always thought so. She's lean with an athletic figure from all the tennis she plays, but she's got some very feminine curves. Great hips. Nice round breasts, not too big, not too small. Fabulous smile. Kim used to swoon over the smile and the cleft in her chin. I don't think Allison liked Kim very much, though. Of course, I love that now. When I was with Kim, it bothered me a little bit, though Allison and I have never talked about it. It's her confidence, though, that draws people to her. She puts on no airs. She is who she is. What you see is what you get with Allison. *That* makes her supremely attractive to others. I am often surprised she's stayed single as long as she has. It's certainly not from lack of prospects.

The same women get a second eyeful as Allison returns to me with our drinks. I watch her approach. She's chosen jeans tonight, as have I. Hers aren't "skinny jeans," per se, but they're tapered at the ankle, and they hug her behind very nicely (I noticed as she went to the bar...so sue me). A black ribbed tank top hugs the rest of her, and she topped it off with a white button-down that she's left open, the sleeves rolled up to mid-forearm. She's taken what could again be considered a rather butch outfit and femmed it up a bit by adding big silver hoop earrings, some bangle bracelets, sandals, toenail polish, and a little lip gloss. I'm not sure how she does it, but Allison has her own very unique style, and it's hot. Very hot. I envy her.

She hands me my drink, which is in a plastic cup, and takes a swig of her beer, also in plastic. I guess they don't want to worry about broken glass on the dance floor. Allison watches me sip. I make a face.

"Wow. They do not skimp on the alcohol here," I say, surprised yet again that my drink isn't watered down.

"I know. I watched her make it," Allison tells me and holds up her own cup. "I'll stick to my beer. At least I know what I'm getting."

We people watch for a few minutes. The dance floor is packed with sweaty, writhing bodies, both male and female. It's a nice mix, and everybody looks happy. I'm reasonably sure the flashing, strobing lights will give me a headache if we're here too long, but for the moment, I'm okay. The music is an eclectic blend of modern house music and eighties dance tunes. When Frankie Goes to Hollywood's *Relax* comes on, Allison gives me a look, all raised eyebrows and huge grin. She takes my drink from my hand and sets it next to her beer on the shelf behind us. Her hand slides down my arm, grasps mine, and she bounces onto the dance floor, tugging me behind her, somehow gaining us enough of a space to dance in regardless of the sardine-like crowd already moving to the music.

I'm not drunk. I'm not even close. But Allison is so much fun to dance with, I can't help but get into it a little. We both love this song, and we sing it at the top of our lungs as we dance, even though our voices are completely drowned out by the music. I am surprisingly into this, I realize suddenly, as I raise my arms over my head and dance like nobody's around. Closing my eyes, I feel the lyrics pour from my mouth, and then Allison is behind me, up against me, her arm around my waist, her hips moving against my backside to the beat, dirty dancing with me like we're fifteen years old and have never heard any song so perfect in all of our young lives. I can just make out her voice near my ear, singing along. And for one, awesome, beautiful moment, all my problems, all my heartache, all my loneliness is gone.

For one awesome, beautiful moment, everything is perfect.

Chapter Eight

I AM SURPRISED TO wake with a clear head. Not because I had a lot to drink last night (I really didn't), but because I half expect my skull to be filled with that cottony feeling of not quite being able to hear completely after being exposed to enormous loudness for a long period of time. But that's not the case. I'm clear. I'm unhungover. The sun is streaming through the windows and warming my face. I can feel the chastity pillows against my back, and the gentle sound of deep and even breathing emanates from the other side of them. I sit up slowly and a smile creeps over my face as I see Allison—seemingly twenty yards away in the ginormous bed—sound asleep. One arm is thrown over her head, her Hard Rock Toronto T-shirt askew across her chest. Her right leg is on top of the blankets and I notice for the first time this trip the green and orange friendship bracelet that encircles her ankle. She told me her niece made it for her. For a long moment, I just sit and watch her sleep. I feel good, despite my pleasantly sore muscles from so much dancing last night, and the thought of coffee elevates my mood even more. I am just beginning to think what a nice way to wake up this all is when I remember.

Today is my wedding day.

The realization is so devastating, it would make complete sense to me if the walls just started crumbling around me. Wouldn't faze me in the least. I flop back down on the bed as the excitement for the morning drains slowly out of me like I'm a pricked water balloon. Allison stretches her arms over her head and groans.

"Oh, my god, my legs are killing me," she says, and her voice has a slight rasp to it, probably from all the singing we did last night. "I am so out of shape. I need to get my ass back to the gym." My lack of response prompts her to sit up and peer over the row of pillows. I feel her eyes on me. "Hey. You okay?"

I simply turn my welled-up eyes to her, and she knows.

"Oh, shit." The pillows are torn out of the way, and she scoots over and the next thing I know, she's hugging me as I'm sobbing into her shirt, cooing comforting sounds to me and kissing the top of my head.

"Goddamn it," I say eventually. "I didn't want to feel this way today. I wanted to have fun, to get drunk, to dance some more, and to scream 'Fuck you, Kim' at the top of my freaking lungs." I say all of this through the tears and snot running down my face, my voice cracking like I'm five years old, and the whole picture just makes me so angry. The combination of angry and crushed is not a pretty one, and for a fleeting moment, I wish Allison didn't have to see me like this.

"Okay. Listen to me." Allison grips my shoulders and pushes me back to almost arm's length so she can look me in the face. "Here's the deal. First of all, you're right. Fuck Kim. She's a bitch. And a coward. And on top of that, she's just stupid and obviously has no freaking taste."

"You think so?" Five-year-old voice again.

"Yes! Totally stupid. Who wouldn't want to marry you?"

"She doesn't."

"Exactly. Stupid. Second, you and I are going to have a great day. We will be together all day long. We'll do fun stuff. We'll have cocktails. I think we should go dancing again because that was a blast. We'll eat like pigs. We'll do everything we can to have a fabulous time, you and me. Fuck Kim. What do you say?"

It occurs to me in that moment that I am unbelievably lucky to have Allison. I truly can't think about what I'd do today if she wasn't here. I try to express my gratitude by throwing my arms around her neck and hugging her as tightly as I can. I feel her arms around my back, her grip solid and sure, and again, I have the weird, unfamiliar sense of being safe in that place. I shake it off and whisper my thanks in her ear.

"You're welcome," she says quietly, and we stay that way for a long while. When I feel like I've pulled myself together—at least a bit—I let her go and reach around her for the box of tissues on the nightstand next to her. As I'm cleaning up my face, she says, "Get in the shower. Relax. Wash off all this residual Kim sadness, and we'll start our day. Okay?"

"Okay." I blow my nose. Loudly, as usual.

Allison smiles and tucks my hair behind my ear. "Go."

I've never been able to meditate or focus in a yoga class. I have too much going on in my head and shutting down my brain takes Herculean effort—something I can't even come close to exerting this morning. I try to concentrate instead on the simple task of showering. I wash my hair, scrubbing with precision. I soap up my body and shave my legs, my arm pits. I neaten up my bikini area and remember how I shaved it all off a while back because that seemed to be the in thing to do, and one of my friends recommended I do it. I actually chuckle now as I remember how stupid that was. I walked around scratching obsessively at my crotch for over a week like I had fleas in my panties. My friend was all, "Oh, you have to shave it every day, and give it time, and it'll stop itching." That was a total lie. It never stopped itching. I wanted to kill somebody. Took me almost a month to grow it all back in. Never again.

See? See how my brain is all over the place? This makes me laugh, too, and for a moment I'm happy because I'd rather be laughing at what a dope I was to shave off all my pubic hair than crying over the fact that I'm supposed to be getting married today.

I finish up and am toweling off when a knock startles me.

"Are you decent?" Allison asks through the bathroom door.

"Hang on." I wrap the big fluffy towel around my body and fasten it at my cleavage, then open the door.

Allison has two champagne flutes in her hand and holds one out to me. "Mimosas to celebrate the awesome day we are about to have."

Warmth floods me as I take my glass. The ping of the flutes touching is almost musical, and we sip.

"There's also coffee out here, and some pastries. Can't have you drunk at nine a.m." She winks at me as she shuts the door, then adds in a god-awful British accent, "Just throw on something comfy for now, as we shall be eating breakfast on the terrace."

With an eye roll, I shake my head and smile, and for the six hundredth time this morning, I thank god for Allison.

My reflection betrays nothing of what today is, what's on my mind. I slept well, so there are no tell-tale dark circles under my eyes. The blue of them is clear, not foggy, though they're a bit red-rimmed from crying. I comb my blonde hair back, detangling it, and not for the first time (or the last, I suspect) I wonder what it is that Kim didn't see in me. I'm not unattractive, really. At least I don't think I am. I have a good face. I drop my towel and inspect myself in the glass. It's a decent body, not too skinny, not too pudgy. I shave. I do my best to smell nice. What am I missing? What does Tina have that I don't?

The lump in my throat tells me I need to curtail this line of thinking right now, so I clear it, swallow hard, and unwrap the cord on the hotel's blow dryer. Once my hair is dry and I've thrown on gym shorts and a T-shirt, I leave the bathroom.

The first thing I notice is the beautiful warmth of the salt-tinged air wafting through our room. Allison has the sliding glass door open, and I am instantly annoyed that I haven't opened it yet in the two days I've been here, because there is nothing so relaxing as the scent of the sea. I inhale as much of it as I can and follow the breeze.

Allison is sitting in one of two metal chairs flanking a round bistro table on the balcony, chewing.

"You made breakfast," I say, no small amount of wonder in my tone.

A plate of croissants sits in the center, a small assortment of jams nearby. Two mugs of coffee steam in the morning air, and I see by the lightened color that mine has already been doctored the way I like it.

"I called room service. Our coffee maker is possessed. I thought it was going to explode." Allison gestures to the empty chair. "Sit. Eat. Relax. We don't have to be anywhere. The day is ours."

I pick up the mug of coffee and hold it in both hands as if worried somebody might steal it from me. The aroma is delicious, and I sip as Allison sits back in her chair and props her feet up on the balcony railing.

"This is the life," she says with a relaxed sigh.

I sit, mimicking her position. We're high up, but can still hear the waves rolling in. The breeze is strong, but not irritatingly so, and the smell of the salt air fills my lungs like a drug. I tear a corner off a croissant, and the buttery pastry nearly melts in my mouth.

"I admit it," I say finally. "I could get used to this."

Allison holds her mug out to me and we cheer, and there's a small part of me that starts to think maybe…just maybe…this will be a good day.

By noon, I'm still doing pretty well, considering. I've itched several times to text Kim, alternately to tell her I miss her and to inform her that I hate her guts. But Allison made me leave my phone in the room, which was probably smart. At least I think so when I'm not jonesing to make contact. It has also occurred to me that Allison's plan for the day is to stuff me full of as much food as she possibly can, as we've been eating since the balcony breakfast and are now sitting down to a late lunch at an outdoor café.

"Only appetizers," I beg. "Something light or you're going to have to roll me back to the room."

Allison chuckles. "Deal."

The last thing we had was ice cream while we wandered the beach, so we decide it's okay to order alcohol now. When our wine arrives, I hold my glass up. "Allison."

"Hm?"

"I know your goal has been to keep me occupied, to keep my mind off the details of today, and I want you to know how much I appreciate it. And our friendship. I don't know what I'd do without you in my life. I love you." It's the god's honest truth, and my eyes fill with tears as I say the words. I know the day's not over, that there is still plenty of time for me to fall apart, but right now, I'm doing okay, and I owe that to her.

Allison's face softens, and I see her eyes sparkle with wetness as well. She seems to study me for a long moment before she replies, "I love you, too, Kenz."

We clink and sip and the moment is broken by a voice closer to our table than either of us realized.

"Hey, Al. Long time, no see." The woman standing near us isn't tall, isn't even close to tall—and I can tell from my seat, so that says a lot. But what she lacks in size, she makes up for in energy, as her presence is practically vibrating the air around us. Short blonde hair and very bronzed skin serve as a frame for the most stunning pair of green eyes I've ever seen in my life. A tattoo of some sort of vine snakes around her wrist and all the way up her arm to her shoulder. She's got at least five earrings in each ear, plus one in her nose, a hoop at the end of her eyebrow, and a silver stud through her bottom lip. I try not to grimace at the thought of all those holes in my face.

"Jules," Allison says, and her face almost lights up. I squint at her. "How are you?"

"I'm great," Jules says, all smiles with a little bit of coy thrown in. "I thought I'd hear from you yesterday." She glances at me, then her eyes flick back to Allison and I think, *Now? Now you wonder who I am? Maybe you should have wondered before you opened your mouth.* Not surprisingly, I decide I don't really care for Jules, though I'm not really sure why.

"Oh, yeah. Sorry about that." Allison doesn't offer an excuse, which I find interesting. And kind of awesome. She holds her hand out and gestures toward me. "This is my good friend, Mackenzie. Kenz, this is Jules. We met Wednesday night."

Ah, now it's clear. While I went back to the room and drowned my sorrows in half a bottle of champagne, Allison was out meeting hot lesbians. That doesn't annoy me. At all. Why should it? I reach out a hand and shake Jules's.

"Are you around tonight?" Jules shifts her weight from one foot to the other, and I suspect she's one of those irritating people who can't stay still for five seconds.

"I'm actually hanging with Kenzie tonight, but we're not sure where we'll be, so maybe we'll run into you?" Allison isn't using her blow-off voice on Jules (I know because I've heard it more than once), and that rankles me a bit. Does she like her? And what am I, her mother with my disapproval and nosy questions?

When Jules nods, she does so from the shoulders up. "That sounds great. I think we'll probably be at Night Moves." I'm pretty sure that's the dance club we were at last night.

"Great. We'll see what we're up for tonight and maybe catch you there."

"Cool." Jules body-nods some more, then gives me a half-hearted wave. "Nice to meet you."

"You, too," I say and watch her go. Then I shift my gaze to Allison and raise my eyebrows in question.

"What?" she asks.

"Who's Jules?"

Allison shrugs it off. "I met her when I went dancing after you went upstairs. Jules is here with some friends, and we hit it off. She bought me a drink. And oh, my god, you should see her dance. Jesus."

"Sounds like she was expecting something a little more from you." I hate the way my voice sounds right now. I try to lighten it with a half-hearted grin, but I don't think it works.

Allison leans her arms on the table and tilts her head to the side, giving me a look that very clearly says, *Really?*

I blow out a breath. "I know. I'm sorry. I don't know what's wrong with me."

The waiter comes to take our order for a hummus plate and the tapenade sampler. When he leaves, Allison is smiling at me.

"What?" I ask.

She gives her head a shake. "Nothing. It's just kind of cute that you want me all to yourself."

I chuckle. "I know! I don't know what's going on with me. I'm sorry. If you want to date Ms. Can't Stay Still, who am I to stand in your way?"

"She does have some nervous energy."

"You think?"

Allison grins, but says, "Seriously. You should see her dance. She's amazing."

"Well, maybe we'll go back there tonight." I shrug. We had a great time last night. There's no reason to think we won't have as good a time tonight. I pick up my wine glass, sip what is actually a very good Sauvignon Blanc, and scope out the room.

It's not busy, probably because it's between lunch and dinner. This café, rather than a nautical motif, is decorated in a more rustic theme. Lots of wood beams and features that have been artificially weathered. The bar looks old and well-worn, and it's trimmed with a brass foot rail and black-upholstered stools. The round tables are covered with tan tablecloths, an uncommon color for such a thing, but a color that ties the seating to the rest of the décor. I like it. It has a cozy, homey feel.

There's not much of a crowd, a handful of people here and there, and I mention that as the waiter arrives with our food.

"Probably because the weather's so nice," Allison says. "People want to be out in the sun, not stuck inside."

I look up from the pita chip I've loaded up with tapenade. "Do you want to be outside?"

"I am perfectly fine right here," she tells me, and her expression is totally sincere. "Besides, it's five days before Christmas. The sunshine and eighty-degree temperatures are kind of freaking me out."

I laugh, and then lean closer to her across the table like I'm going to tell her a secret. "Me, too! It's *so weird*."

"I never thought I'd miss snow and cold," Allison says, her voice low. "But I do. I feel like I'm in the wrong place. And putting a Santa hat on a flamingo doesn't help. It just makes it weirder."

"I totally agree," I whisper. Then, "Why are we whispering?"

We both burst into laughter at that, and I suddenly realize how very content I feel at this moment, regardless of what the day is—or what the day was supposed to be—and I order us each another glass of wine.

"I love Christmas," Allison says, her voice wistful. "The spirit of the season. The way everybody's a little bit nicer, a little bit more patient. My grandma is a huge fan of the holidays. She always talks about the magic."

Our wine arrives. "The magic?" I ask as I sip.

"It's kind of corny, I guess." Allison shrugs. "She always talked about Christmas magic. I know now that she was referring to that stuff that happens during the holidays: the way everybody is a little kinder, a little nicer, a bit more considerate. But back then, I had no idea. And she has this snow globe collection. I could never keep my hands off it as a kid. I always had to shake them all. I'd do it as fast as I could to see if I could get all of them snowing at once."

The image of ten-year-old Allison warms me. "Could you?"

"Not after she kept buying them." Her laugh is a deep rumble. "You try shaking twenty-seven snow globes as fast as possible. See how successful you are. Anyway, she'd always tell me to keep shaking them because I was releasing the Christmas magic into the air, and the more, the better."

"I love that," I say, and we hold each other's gaze. Looking down, I exhale. "I feel like my life is a snow globe right now. All picture perfect and pretty, but then some kid has come along and shaken the shit out of it."

Laughter overtakes us both. When we recover ourselves, Allison says, "It's just the magic being released. Hang onto something. It'll be okay." She lifts her glass. "To snow globes."

"And Christmas magic," I add.

We clink.

Chapter Nine

AT 3:55, SLIGHTLY BUZZED and having an amazing time, Allison and I arrive at the massage suite.

"So, how does this work?" Allison asks, her dark brows furrowing above her nose.

"I booked us a couple's massage," I tell her with a bit of a giggle. "But I've never had one. I have no idea how it works."

Allison grins and shakes her head.

I shrug. "I mean, I know it's for *couples* couples, but I thought it'd be fun. And the massage I got yesterday was incredible."

"I guess we'll find out."

I grab her hand and tug her through the door behind me. Rob is at the desk once again, and he gives me a big smile.

"You're back," he says.

"I am. We have an appointment for four."

Rob scans his computer screen and nods. "Yup. I have you set up for a couple's massage with Stella and Frankie." My hesitation must have shown on my face because he lowers his voice and adds, "Frankie is a she. No worries."

He leads us to a room further down the hall than the one I was in yesterday. It's bigger, but has the same ambiance—though thank god, no patchouli. It smells more like vanilla, and it's warm and inviting. There are two beds side by side, but with enough space between them for a body to move.

"One on each bed, obviously," Rob says. "Take off whatever you feel comfortable having off and scoot under the blanket. The girls will be in in a few minutes." He flashes a smile and leaves us alone.

"I don't know if you've had a massage before," I say to Allison, who is standing next to one of the beds and looking uncertain. "But I take off everything but my underwear. They can't really do a good job on your back with your bra in the way."

"Oh. Okay. Cool." She starts to disrobe immediately, and her total lack of modesty makes me grin. Only when I start to take my clothes off does she turn from me and face the other direction. I take a quick second to admire the planes of her back before I do the same and give her privacy, stripping down to my hot pink panties. We do a weird backwards walk so that we can each slide under our respective blankets without facing each other, and in a few quick moments, we're both in position with our faces in the little donut-shaped head rests. Before I can say anything at all to Allison, there's a soft knock at the door.

"All set?" I recognize Stella's voice and affirm that they can come in. "Is this your first time having a couple's massage?"

"Well, yes," I say, "But we're not actually a couple. We're friends. Best friends."

"Even better," Stella says as she walks near the head of my bed so I can see her feet.

"Different socks this time," I comment as I take in the rainbow stripes.

"I've learned it's better to change them every day." We both chuckle at that. "Who's doing who here?"

"Oh," I say, and I've actually thought about this. "I'd like you, Stella, to take care of Allison. You did such a lovely job on me yesterday, I want to share that with her."

"Sounds good," she says, then, "A little pressure on you, Frankie."

"I'm up to the challenge," Frankie says, speaking for the first time. Her voice is gentle, but there's something strong about it. Confident. It gives me a tingle.

"All right, we'll get started then."

If Stella was good, Frankie is outstanding. Her hands are strong, and she's not using her full strength on me, I can tell. She's holding back a bit, but her fingers know just where to go, just what muscles need extra attention. I know I joked with Stella about making noise during a massage, but I have to make an extra effort not to groan in delight as Frankie kneads my calf muscle, gently, firmly, gently, until I feel like it's made of Jell-O. Then she switches to the other one. After a minute or two working that leg, I am sure I'm melting right into the bed, like the Wicked Witch of the West in *The Wizard of Oz* after Dorothy throws water on her. The witch's voice—*I'm melting!*—zips through my head, and I roll my lips in and bite down on them to keep from laughing out loud.

The room is quiet aside from the soft pan flute music coming through the speakers mounted in the ceiling. I don't want to disturb the peace, yet at the same time, I wonder how Allison is doing. I decide to throw caution (and etiquette) to the wind.

"Hey, Al, how's it going over there?"

Allison groans loudly, and all three of us chuckle at her. "Oh, my god," Allison says, and I can tell she's talking through her teeth. "I'm thinking of asking Stella to marry me."

"I'm sure she never gets that offer here."

"What's it up to now, Stel?" Frankie asks. "Twelve? Thirteen marriage proposals?"

"It's around that," Stella says, modestly I think.

"And what about you?" Frankie asks, and I can tell she's talking to me because she gives my shoulder a squeeze. "Am I living up to Stella's standards?"

"Absolutely," I manage to breathe as she works on my upper back. Her fingers dance over my skin, and I'm in heaven. Gently, she brushes my hair off the back of my neck and off to the side, then returns to my neck, kneading and pressing the muscles there. Her fingers work into my hair, along my scalp, and the tingling sensation I've been feeling suddenly focuses lower in my body. I swallow, keep my eyes closed, and instead of wondering if this touch is acceptable massage therapist behavior (it feels slightly more intimate than the rest of my massage), just simply revel in the feel of being touched by another woman.

Then something weird happens. I don't know how, and I don't know why, but it's as if some door or lid has been opened by Frankie's hands, and the pleasure I was feeling mere seconds ago shifts to something more...emotional. I realize belatedly—and with horror—that I'm going to cry, that there's no stopping it. I do my best to stay silent, not to make a sound. I don't want Frankie to think she's hurting me. I don't want Allison to worry. I don't want Stella to think I'm a freak. But the dam cracks just enough for my eyes to fill, and I blink rapidly, then watch as a tear, then two, spatter on the carpet below my head.

I'm supposed to be married by now.

The thought comes unbidden, and I'm astonished to realize that it's the first time I've had that thought since we left the room this morning. While I'm annoyed and a little angry to have it encroach upon such a wonderful experience, I also know it's to be expected. It's almost five. The wedding was scheduled for three. If everything had gone as planned, I would be Kim's wife right this very second, drinking champagne, dancing, deliriously happy. The lump in my throat feels like a golf ball, and I work hard to swallow it down. I close my eyes again, focus on my breathing, and try not to let the anger and sorrow take over.

It's not easy.

I only have to hang on for another minute or two before I feel the blanket pulled back up over my body.

"Take as much time as you want," Stella says, and a second or two later, the door opens and clicks shut. Silence reigns for a long moment before Allison speaks.

"You okay?"

I nod before I realize that she can't see me. I hear her move.

"Kenz?"

"I'm good," I say, keeping my face in the donut hole, listening to the rustle of fabric as Allison gets up and, I assume, begins to dress.

"Are you sure? You weren't a minute ago."

I lift my head, look at her. She's in her shorts and bra, her arms in the sleeves of her shirt. Her face is flushed, like she just had a good nap. Or a good orgasm. "How do you know?"

She gestures to the floor with her eyes. "I could see your tears."

I blow out a huge breath and sit up, holding the blanket over my bare chest. "Yeah, I don't know what happened."

Allison gives me a half shrug. "Massages release toxins and other crap in your muscles. Sometimes, that opens up other channels. Emotional ones. I don't think crying is uncommon."

"Really? Okay, that makes me feel a tiny bit less like a giant dork."

"You're not a dork."

I turn my back to her, sit up, put on my bra. "Do you think they knew?"

"Who?"

"Stella and Frankie?"

"I don't know. If they did, I'm sure they weren't surprised. I doubt you're the first."

When we're dressed, we head out to the reception area where Rob awaits with his 1500 watt smile. I'm relieved to see no sign of Stella nor Frankie. We pay and leave tips and are on our way.

Allison drops her arm around my shoulders and pulls me close against her as we walk.

I take a deep breath, snuggle into her for a second. "It was weird. It was the first time since this morning that I'd thought about what today is—supposed to be—and I just think it caught me off guard. Plus, Frankie had her hand in my hair and it felt…" I shake my head, unable to verbalize my thoughts.

Allison gives me a look. "I didn't get the hair massage."

I bump her with my hip. "Well, you must not be as special as I am."

"I guess not." We walk along for a moment. "Where to next?"

"I want to get drunk," I say, surprising myself.

"Yeah?"

"Yeah. Fuck it. It's my wedding day. If I'm not getting married, then I should at least be able to get good and plastered."

Allison gives me a grin. "How about we go out drinking and dancing and have fun and not make 'getting plastered' an actual goal?"

"It could happen."

"It definitely could."

"It *should* happen."

"I don't know about that."

My eyes roll before I can stop them. "Okay, Fun Police. Can we go get a drink at least?" I punctuate my maturity by bouncing on the balls of my feet like a toddler in a toy store.

Allison eyes me. I know what she's thinking because we read each other so well. She's giving me her stern face, and I accept that she's going to be watching me tonight. Closely. I don't care. I don't give a shit. I want to get drunk. Is that so much to ask?

"Yes," she says finally, still looking at me. "If that's what you want. Let's go get a drink."

Chapter Ten

I'M NOT DRUNK, BUT I'm damn close. Another cocktail or two, and I'll be right in the perfect spot between 'happily drunk' and 'time to ease up.' The rum runners are ridiculously delicious, and I order another one at the bar, not needing to shout over the music because the handsome bartender is already very familiar with me.

Allison sits on the barstool next to my hip sipping her Diet Coke. She stopped drinking about an hour ago. Two drinks ago for me. We're at the same club we were before. Night Moves. What a stupid name. What is this, 1976? It's okay, though, because the music is pumping, bodies are churning on the dance floor, and I am feeling no pain. Not even from the text that was on my phone when we got back to the room earlier. The text from Kim.

Thinking about u today. Hope ur all right. Miss u.

I stood and blinked at it until Allison came and took it out of my hands.

"Are you fucking kidding me?" she snapped, her eyes flashing with anger. "What's the matter with her? And can't she spell?" She tossed the phone onto the bed and looked at me. My eyes were full. Of course they were. I knew it and so did Allison. She opened her arms and took me into her embrace just in time for me to burst into a full-on meltdown, sobbing like a child. Allison held me while I cried—I have no idea how long I went on—and didn't let go even when I'd subsided down to those little hiccups that you get when you're just about done falling apart. She kissed the top of my head, stroked my hair, my back, and murmured the things you say to somebody who couldn't be any more upset. I don't know how much time passed before she loosened her embrace so she could look me in the face.

"Hey," she said, and waited until my eyes met hers. "Fuck her."

I swallowed. I nodded.

"No," Allison said, her dark brows pointed down in anger, her voice steely. "Fuck. Her. I mean it."

I nodded again.

"You know what?" she asked. "I'm glad she's gone. I'm glad she dumped you. You know why? Because you deserve better. You. Deserve. Better. Understand me?"

It wasn't often that I saw Allison so determined, so set. So angry. I nodded a third time.

"Say it," she ordered me, her hands gripping my shoulders.

"I deserve better."

"Yes, you do." She pulled me to her and hugged me again. "Yes. You do."

"Can we go get a drink now?" I asked, my voice muffled against her shirt.

She chuckled. "Absolutely."

And here we are. Dancing. Shouting to be heard. As I grab my drink from the bartender, Allison gives me a look I can't read, but I'm not sure if it's because it's an unusual look or because I'm too intoxicated to read her accurately.

"What?" I ask her.

She shakes her head. "Nothing."

I'm about to ask her again when blonde hair catches my eye. I groan, though I try to do it quietly. "You have a visitor," I say and hope my smile doesn't look forced.

Allison looks over her shoulder just in time for Jules to wrap her in a hug.

"Hi," she says to Allison, though she stretches the one syllable into about four, like she's breathing life onto Allison. I wonder if Jules has had as much to drink as I have. Allison doesn't seem the least bit turned off. The opposite, actually. I roll my eyes and turn away from the display, scanning the crowd and drinking my rum runner in swallows that are way too big. I know it. I just can't seem to help it. Big swallows keep thoughts of Kim away. I don't know why. Don't ask me.

As I have been since I arrived at The Rainbow's Edge, I am once again struck by the enormous mix of people, this time on the dance floor. People of all shapes, sizes, genders, colors, and dancing talent cram the parquet and move as if they make up one giant, breathing, gyrating form. I'm torn between pushing my way into the middle of it all and staying where I am, an observer on the outside.

"Here you go." The voice is right next to my ear, intimately close. A new drink appears in front of my face as if by magic. It's another rum runner. I turn to meet eyes that are such a light blue they're nearly transparent. They're part of a face I don't know, and my expression says so.

She's incredibly attractive, especially when she smiles. Her short, dark hair is swept to the side, then spiked in the front. She's dressed in tight black jeans, a gray V-neck T-shirt, and a black leather vest. "You don't recognize me, do you?"

The voice seems vaguely familiar, but it's so loud in here that I can't focus on it clearly. I shake my head.

"Maybe this will help." Before I know what's going on, she grasps the back of my neck with her hand and begins to knead the muscles there, working up into my hair. That's when I know.

"Frankie?"

Her grin widens, revealing even teeth. I take a moment to look at her, since I didn't have the chance during my massage. She's taller than I am, powerfully built. The outfit definitely accentuates that, as does her posture. There's something…confident about the way she stands. I glance at her hands, noting the power in them as well, and the quick flash I have of them on my body earlier sends a jolt straight to my groin. Her lips are thin, her jaw square, and there's a scar near her left eyebrow that I have the urge to run my fingertips over.

Her eyes indicate my drink. "Thought you could use a refill."

I thank her, but then a thought occurs to me, and I squint at her. "Wait a minute. How did you know who I was? You didn't see my face at all during my massage."

She moves a little closer. "I watched you leave. Closed circuit cameras monitor the reception area. I checked you out when you left."

My eyebrows raise. "You checked me out?"

Frankie nods and sips her drink. It's clear and has a lime wedge in it.

"Why?"

"I wanted to see what kind of face went with that hot body and gorgeous hair."

She says it so matter-of-factly that I'm speechless for a moment. Forward and flattering. That's what it is. And weirdly arousing. I take another gulp of my drink. "And?"

"It's the whole package. Absolutely."

I can't help the grin that spreads across my face, though I try to keep it more 'coy' than 'oh-my-god-she-said-I-have-a-hot-body.' I'm not sure I succeed, but I thank her and drink some more.

"Wanna dance?"

"Okay."

She takes my nearly-empty cup and sets it on a nearby table with hers, then holds out her hand to me. I take it, her grip warm and strong, and let her lead me onto the dance floor.

I'm not familiar with the song that's playing, but the beat is steady and the bass is thumping, and it's easy to move to. Frankie's hand slips around to the small of my back and she pulls me in close. I normally wouldn't dance like this with somebody I just met. Hell, I normally wouldn't dance at all. But the rum runners have done their job, and I abruptly realize that I'm awfully close to drunk. So when Frankie pushes her knee between my legs and dances really close to me, I let her. In fact, I help her. I get into it. Why not? This is a sexy woman, and she thinks I'm hot.

Fuck you, Kim.

That's what runs through my head just seconds before I clasp my hands around the back of Frankie's neck and let the music take me.

We dance like that—close and hot and sexy—for two more songs before we're both out of breath and decide drink refills are in order. When we get them, Frankie leans in close.

"I've got to hit the john," she says, her breath tickling my ear. "Don't go away." And then I think the tip of her tongue flicks the ridge of my ear. I *think* it does. I stare as she gives me a wink and heads in the direction of the bathrooms.

"Who the hell is that?" Allison's voice startles me so much that I swallow wrong. It takes me several seconds and a couple good thumps on the back from Allison before I can breathe again.

"Jesus," I say, gulping air.

"Who was that?" Allison's tone is odd.

I grin. "*That* is Frankie." At her blank look, I elaborate. "From the massage?"

Allison blinks twice. "Seriously? How did she know it was you?"

I explain the closed circuit security camera. "She thought I had a hot body." I almost giggle as I say it. "She wanted to see my face."

"That's kind of creepy."

I push playfully at her. "It is not."

"It kind of is, Kenz. And you're drunk."

"It is not. I mean, I am not."

"Really? How many of those have you had?"

"A few."

"Uh-huh."

I don't like the disapproval in her eyes. It confuses me, but I don't know if that's because I'm actually confused or if she's right, and I'm just drunk. I decide to counter-attack. "Where's your little blonde pin cushion?"

Allison tilts her head to one side. "Really?"

I shrug. "Just asking."

"She's at the end of the bar with her friends. We've been dancing."

"Good for you."

Allison's body language changes, and she moves in closer to me. "Seriously, Mackenzie, you don't find it a little creepy that Frankie works here and was checking you out after your massage?"

I shake my head, then try to steady it with one hand. "No. Why should I?"

"It makes the hair massage a little weirder, don't you think?" When I don't answer, she steps back slightly, stands up straighter. "I don't know. I would just wonder how often she does that. How many other clients she's 'checked out.'" She makes air quotes with her fingers.

The cup in my hand is empty. I stare at it, blink a couple times, uncertain how that happened. Yeah, I'm drunk. Really drunk. I am aware of it now. And I'm angry. I don't like Allison's judgment. I lift my head to look at her, and it takes my vision an extra second to catch up. "It's my goddamn wedding day, Allie, and my girlfriend is off someplace else, probably fucking her ex while I am on our honeymoon without her. Forgive me if I have a few drinks too many. Shoot me if I think it's flattering that somebody finds me attractive. So what if I want to dance with her all night long? If it takes my mind off of my broken heart, then that's what I'm going to do. Is that okay with you?"

Allison goes very still, but her blue eyes stay hooked to mine. She blinks a couple times, swallows, licks her lips, then gives one nod. "Yeah. Okay. It's fine with me. Just...be careful." With that, she turns away and heads back to where I can just make out Jules and a few others, all laughing and seeming to have a great time.

Before I can think too much more, a hand touches my back.

"Miss me?" Frankie asks.

"Yes," I say with determination. I grab her hand. "Let's dance some more. Then I want another drink." I lead her onto the dance floor, and this time, I push *my* knee between *her* legs as we start to move to the beat.

Frankie is incredibly sexy. This becomes more and more obvious as the night wears on. We dance, we drink, we flirt. I notice that she flirts with a lot of women, even the ones she seems to know well. I assume those are other employees.

"What's it like to work here?" I ask her during one of our drink breaks. I have no idea how many rum runners I've had, but I think it's somewhere in the neighborhood of fifty.

Frankie shrugs, her blue eyes focused on nothing as she scans the crowd. "It's cool. I mean, what gay person doesn't want to work someplace where they're surrounded by other gay people?"

"And where do you live? In town somewhere?"

"There's a wing here, off on the east side of the resort, where all the employees are housed."

"Really?" It sounds so cool to me, like a TV show. "You have an apartment here?"

Frankie gives a snort. "No. It's not quite that awesome. We each have a room and a roommate. The work is kind of seasonal, so we don't all live here all the time."

"Where do you live when you don't live here?"

"Around," she says with a noncommittal shrug.

We dance some more, and I am *really* intoxicated. Frankie is doing all the leading now, I'm just kind of going with her, mimicking her moves. I don't feel great. My eyes scan for Allison, but I can't seem to focus on anything, so I stop trying and let the music take me. I have no idea what the song is. I have no idea how much time has passed. I have no idea of much of anything except the thumping bass in the pit of my stomach and Frankie's warm hand pressed against my back.

The crowd has thinned. I do notice that. "What time is it?" I ask. At least I think I say it out loud.

"Why?" Frankie asks. "You want to go back to your room?" There's a twinkle in her eye.

"You're sexy," I think, but notice too late that I actually say it out loud.

She gives me that mischievous smile. "So are you. Come on." She leads me to the bar and orders me a glass of water. I drink it down in one try as she tucks my hair behind my ear. "I want to show you something," she tells me, then reaches inside her vest.

When she pulls her hand out, she's holding what looks like a piece of a plant. I furrow my brows in confusion, but when she holds it up over my head, something clicks.

Mistletoe.

She's kissing me before I even realize it, and then I'm kissing her back before I can think better of it. But why should I think better of it? I deserve this. I try not to think about how differently than Kim she kisses, how much more demanding her mouth is than Kim's ever was. I always took the lead when Kim and I made out. She always followed me. So having somebody else driving this kiss is...different. Not in a bad way, but in a new way. Frankie pushes her tongue into my mouth. I use mine to duel with her.

Fuck you, Kim.

There it is again. The thought of the day. I grab Frankie's head in both my hands and put everything I've got into this kiss. Which isn't as much as usual because of the six dozen cocktails in my system. I feel my balance shift, and then Frankie is laughing and keeping me from falling over right there in the club.

"Whoopsie," I say, then wonder who on earth actually says that.

"Where's your room?" Frankie asks.

"I'm on the Honeymoon Floor," I tell her, and even *I* think I'm slurring my words. Not a good sign.

Frankie stops, looks at me. "But...you said you're not with that other chick. Didn't you?"

I wave my hand dismissively and just miss smacking us both in the face. "Oh, I'm not. I'm not. She's a friend. See, my ex left me for *her* ex, so I decided to take the honeymoon anyway. Fuck her."

Frankie laughs, and if she's wary of me now, I don't see it. "Yeah, fuck her. She's obviously an idiot."

"She totally is. Let's go."

"Just give me one second," Frankie says. "I'll be right back."

It's not as obvious to me in the club as it is once we leave how much I need Frankie's support to walk. My focus is off. My eyes won't seem to stay on one thing for very long. I'm having trouble getting my feet to work. I have to squeeze my eyes closed during the entire elevator ride, and I work really hard willing myself not to throw up. Oh, my god, how much did I drink? I think I asked the question out loud, but since neither Frankie nor any of the other people in the elevator answer me, I decided I must not have. Weirdly, I have a bottle of water in my hand, and I have no idea how it got there. It occurs to me to drink some, but I don't. I think I don't. I'm not sure.

After that, time seems to start skipping on me because the next thing I know, we're at the door to my room. "Where's my water?" I ask (I *think* I ask out loud). My hands are empty, but nobody answers me. I blink, hard, and try to remember actually walking down the hall, but nothing comes to me. It's a complete blank. Elevator. Door to my room. There's nothing in between, which freaks me out a bit. Frankie's arm is around my waist, and she's making a noise that sounds like effort, so I have to think she's probably holding me up. I'm not sure. My room key suddenly appears, but I don't recall giving it to her.

At that moment, the floor tilts, and I squeeze my eyes shut. When I open them, I'm in the room and lying face down on my bed. I lift my head, which turns out to be an absolutely terrible idea, and a groan rumbles out of me. I let my face drop back into the comforter and begin taking inventory of my body parts. I move each leg. I wiggle my fingers. That's about it. I have no desire to move anything else. Except my mouth feels like it's stuffed with cotton and a glass of water would be heavenly. I lift my head again when I hear movement, try to form words that at least somewhat resemble the word 'water,' but it sounds more like some weird form of muffled mumbling. My head drops again, and I whimper.

I am just beginning to zero in on exactly how stupid I am when all sound fades out, and my world goes black.

Chapter Eleven

SUNSHINE IS NOT ALWAYS AWESOME.

Sometimes it's cruel.

Like this morning, as it stabs into my eyelid, feeling very much like a needle. Or a knife. Or a sword. Or a machete. Something big. And sharp. And mean.

Not surprisingly, my head is pounding like somebody has taken up residence inside my skull. Somebody with a ballpeen hammer. Right now, that person is focused just above my eyes, around my forehead, pounding away. I want to open my eyes, to look around and make sure I'm not lying out in the open, on the deck near the pool or something equally embarrassing, but I'm afraid. I'm afraid of the pain. I'm afraid of what I might see. Of who I might see.

My mouth tastes like ass. It's very obvious that I threw up at some point, but since it doesn't feel like I'm lying in a pool of my own vomit, I surmise I must have made it to the bathroom, though I have no recollection of that trip whatsoever.

I take a mental bodily inventory, trying to ascertain my physical well-being by feel only, without opening my eyes. I wiggle my fingers and toes. They seem okay. I'm in a bed. It's cushy underneath me, and I'm covered. I am also naked, which alarms me so much that my eyes pop open.

Mistake.

"Jesus Christ," I mutter and bang my eyes closed again. Not that they literally bang, but it sure as hell feels like it. The quick glimpse I got of my surroundings was enough to reasonably reassure me that I am in my own room, and the relief I feel is a little bit frightening. But last night seems to be a big black hole in my memory, and that is beyond frightening. It's freaking me out.

I try to focus. Concentrate on what I remember last.

The nightclub. Dancing. Drinking. At the thought of a rum runner, my stomach lurches, and for a horrifying moment, I worry I may have to actually drag myself out of this bed and to the bathroom, which will never happen given the rubbery feeling of my legs. If I never see, smell, or taste another drop of rum, it will be too soon.

I don't like this. I've been drunk before. Of course I have. I've even been *very* drunk before. Extremely drunk. Wasted. But I've never had a complete black-out. I've never had no recollection whatsoever of what happened the previous night. The thought of the giant blank spot in my brain is sending me into panic mode.

I try again. Squeeze my eyes shut tight. Focus on the nightclub. Avoid thinking about anything in a plastic cup.

Dancing. Thumping bass (imagining that is not really much of a stretch). Mistletoe.

Mistletoe?

Frankie!

"Oh, my god!" I bolt upright to a sitting position as Frankie's face comes crashing through into my memory. "Oh, my god," I say again, then cover my face with my hands. "Oh, my god. Oh, my god. Oh, my god." I still can't seem to grab at more than bits and pieces from last night, but I am sure Frankie was there. I'm sure she had mistletoe. I'm sure she kissed me. And I'm sure I was a sloppy, drunken mess.

"Oh, Mackenzie," I whisper into my empty room. "Way to embarrass yourself."

I take a deep slow breath and gingerly move my legs to the side of the bed. Ballpeen Hammer Man is going to town on my skull cap now, and keeping my eyes open is painful. Literally. Somehow, I manage to stand upright without toppling over—a feat of which I am stupidly proud. I look back at the bed, and it occurs to me that two things are missing: a giant stain from me puking (thank god) and the row of chastity pillows, which makes me wonder where Allison was last night.

"Probably with the blonde pincushion," I say aloud and shake my head.

Mistake.

I grab both sides of my head and stay very still for long moments. When the wave of nausea passes, I concentrate like a four-year-old trying to write her name, on shuffling my feet, one in front of the other, until I reach the bathroom.

With a hand flat over my eyes, I flick the light switch. Then I slowly spread my fingers, one by one, letting the light in a teeny bit at a time until my brutalized eyeballs grow accustomed to it, and I'm sure I'm not going to hurl. Only then do I remove my hand altogether.

The bathroom is surprisingly clean. As I wonder why I'm surprised, my brain tosses me a flash of a kneeling-down view of the toilet bowl as I expelled everything I possibly could have, and maybe a vital organ or two. I remember gripping the seat for dear life, my hair held back by gentle hands.

"What an impressive first date I make," I say to the empty bathroom. "How the hell am I going to apologize to Frankie? God, I'm such an asshole."

I walk all the way in, sit, and relieve myself, my face buried in my hands as I do so. It occurs to me that maybe this should be my new permanent stance: hands over my face so I never have to look anybody in the eye again. So I never have to look Frankie in the eye again.

I flush, strategically avoid the mirror (I'm not ready for that yet), and go back into the room to get dressed. I'm too battered to actually choose an outfit—and that's how I feel: like I've been in some sort of physical altercation and lost—so I grab a nearby pair of gym shorts and a red T-shirt of Allison's that's on the floor in a heap. My timing is perfect because as soon as I pull the shirt over my head, I hear the clicking of a key card in the door.

Allison looks fresh and amazing, as always, and I briefly entertain the thought of punching her right in the face. Luckily, I don't have the energy. Also, she's holding two steaming cups of coffee, so all my animosity flies out the window.

"My savior," I exclaim as she hands one over. Freshly brewed coffee is the only aroma I can think of smelling that won't make me want to upchuck, and I greedily inhale from its opening.

"Hey, why was the blonde's belly button sore?"

I shrug, not even attempting a guess.

"Because her boyfriend was blonde too."

I snort.

"How're you feeling?" Allison asks, her smile gentle.

"Oh, my god, Al. I am such a loser. Did you see Frankie? Was she here when you got here?"

Allison looks puzzled. "Frankie?"

I sigh and shake my head. "I got trashed last night. Like, really trashed. Like, stupidly, embarrassingly, I-might-end-up-on-*World's Dumbest* trashed. I don't know how it happened. Those damn rum runners. I should know better." I'm talking kind of fast—and half to myself—but Allison is just looking at me, her eyebrows raised in expectation, so I go on. "I was dancing with Frankie, and she had mistletoe, and she kissed me. Wow, did she kiss me." I take an extra second or two to search my memory banks and relive that moment. "Then...it was like I hit a wall or something. A wall of alcohol. A wall of intoxication. All of a sudden, I was just wrecked. And Frankie brought me back here and I got sick—though I'm not sure how many times—and she held my hair and undressed me and put me to bed, but she wasn't here when I woke up."

Allison's expression is one I can't quite read, but I am well aware of my senses being a bit off, so I just sip my coffee.

"I need to find her today and try to apologize. God, I'm so embarrassed." I glance out the window at the ocean, the palm trees waving in the breeze. "I had to be such a turn-off." Something occurs to me, and I turn back to Allison. "Where were you last night? With Jules?" I wink at her, hoping it comes off playful.

Nodding slowly, Allison smiles at me. "Yeah. We were out late, and I was tired, so a bunch of us crashed in her room."

I sip my coffee again, then hold up the cup. "Thanks for this, by the way. It's hitting the spot."

"Good."

"I need to find her. I need to find Frankie. What's the best way to do that, do you think?"

Allison seems to ponder my question. "I guess I'd start at the massage office," she suggests. "Listen, I was going to go hang by the pool for a while. Want to come?"

"Can I meet you there?" I ask. "I really need to take care of this or it's going to drive me crazy."

Allison lifts one shoulder in a half-shrug. "Sure." Then she gathers her pool items and excuses herself to the bathroom.

I open the sliding glass door and step out onto the balcony. The breeze is warm, salty, and I close my eyes, inhale deeply. I'm starting to feel somewhat human, but I know I'm in dire need of water and some aspirin. I vow that as soon as Allison is out of the bathroom, I'll fix myself up as best I can, pull my shit together, and go find Frankie to offer up my sincerest apologies. In the meantime, I pray that no obscure memories from last night pop out at me, as I don't know I can take any more mortifying revelations about my behavior. As it is, I'd rather crawl under a rock than go searching for somebody who was probably so disgusted by me, she ran as soon as she had the chance. But I can't stand the idea of somebody like Frankie thinking my persona last night was a normal occurrence for me. I don't know why it's so important for me to remedy this, and I don't really want to take the time to analyze it. I mean, it's not like Frankie and I are going to get married. We're not dating, obviously. I'm less than three weeks out of a relationship. But the idea of somebody thinking I'm a falling down drunk…I can't take it.

Allison exits the bathroom, dressed in her bathing suit and cover-up, big sunglasses on her face.

"Pretty bright in here," I joke.

She smiles, shoulders her tote bag. "Okay. See you down there?"

I nod as the door closes behind her. I hit the deadbolt so housekeeping doesn't surprise me. Or more accurately, isn't frightened by the sight of me.

I enter the bathroom and am horrified by the woman looking back at me. She's so hideously disheveled that for a split second, I think somebody else is in the room with me. Some stranger with huge bags under her eyes and the nest of a small woodland creature on her head.

"Jesus Christ," I mutter. "How did Allison not scream in terror and run back into the hallway?" It's a legitimate question.

I strip back out of my makeshift PJ's and step into the shower, making the water as hot as I can possibly stand it. I feel dirty, inside and out. I fill my mouth with water, swish it around, spit it out. Bracing my hands against the wall, I let the near-scalding water pound the flesh between my shoulder blades. It hurts. It also feels good, like I'm purging.

As the water pummels me, short flashes zip through my mind, like little bursts of light in a dark cave. Me stumbling through the door to my room, and strong hands keeping me from falling on my face. Kneeling on the bathroom floor, watching as a colorful array of half-digested food and drink rush from my mouth into the toilet bowl. Me muttering, "You're so sexy," in a slur reminiscent of old Red Skelton skits.

"Oh, my god…" Slowly, I drop my forehead against the tile wall between my hands over and over and over.

I stay in the shower until my skin is red. I don't know how much time has passed, but it's long enough for me to have a good cry. I wonder if my period is due soon…I only cry at the drop of a hat during PMS, but maybe it's warranted after last night. After yesterday. For the very first time this morning, I remember what yesterday was. I think that gives the tears the final push they need.

Anyway. I get out, blow my nose, then immediately down two glasses of water (realizing belatedly that Florida tap water is disgusting) and a handful of ibuprofen. Then I go to work brushing my teeth. Between leftover vomit and coffee, I'm sure my breath is a deadly weapon at this point. I brush and try not to look at my reflection. I'm clean now, but the bags are still there, my cheeks seem sunken in, and my eyes seem a bit…lost.

I wander into the room naked, brushing my teeth with an effort I would use if scrubbing sand off them. Hell, they feel like they have sand on them. I stay far enough into the room so nobody outside can see me, but I stare out the open screen door to the ocean below, and a weird feeling of melancholy seems to seep into me. A sadness. A loneliness. For the fiftieth time since I arrived, I think, *This isn't how I'm supposed to be here*. I should be celebrating right now. I should be blissfully content right now. Being hung over today is fine, but I'm supposed to be happy about it, not miserable. Not embarrassed. Not standing here with amnesia about half the night.

My eyes well up, which not only irritates me, but fills my nose with snot, which makes it impossible to breathe with my mouth full of toothpaste lather. I hurry to the bathroom and spit, rinse, then go to work on my hair, which takes longer than it should. I absently wonder if I rolled around in maple syrup or something, given the number of tangles in it. Then I decide I don't really want to know.

Nearly two hours after I first stepped into the shower, I feel like I'm about as presentable as I'm going to get. I'm too exhausted to bother blowing my hair dry. I can't muster the energy to even apply mascara. I've opted for simple and comfortable today, because frankly, I'm too hung over to give a shit what people think of my outfit. Which is very unusual for me. Allison would be proud. I'm wearing my black Under Armour nylon shorts with the white stripe, shorts I usually reserve for hanging around the house and wearing on bike rides. A plain white T-shirt on top is as complicated as it gets. Black flip flops top off the ensemble. Fancy! It suddenly occurs to me that I'm starving. I've gulped down an entire bottle of water that Allison must have left for me, as well as finishing my coffee, so now I just feel full of liquid. I grab my little cross-body bag and my sunglasses (I *know* I'm going to need them) and head off to find food and my savior from last night.

Chapter Twelve

WHAT IS IT ABOUT bacon and eggs that make it such a perfect food combination, good for all occasions? They are my go-to dinner when I don't feel like figuring something else out to cook. They are the best snack food ever invented. And they are the only thing I can keep down after a night of too much alcohol.

I'm sitting in the little café by myself, which is actually kind of nice. I've been in restaurants before, seen people sitting by themselves, reading the paper or a novel, and I've been sad for them. I've assumed they have nobody to eat with. It never occurred to me that maybe they *want* to be eating alone. Maybe they *prefer* it. Like I do right now. I don't even really want to talk to the waitress, though I do…just because I want to be alone, that's no reason to be rude.

I'm not really the kind of person who likes to be alone. I like it better when I'm around people, but I don't know if that's an honest character trait of my personality or if it means I don't enjoy being alone with my own thoughts. I try not to analyze it too much. Right now is different, though, somehow. Maybe it's paranoia. I'm pretty sure the table in the corner with three women that I passed when I walked in were whispering about me and staring. I don't think I've ever seen them before. But since I have a chunk of about four hours I can't seem to remember, who knows? Maybe we had an in-depth conversation last night, the gang of us, and now they think I'm being snooty and ignoring them.

I sip my coffee and watch the comings and goings of the customers, mostly because I've got no idea what my next move is. I need to find Frankie, to (hopefully) make sure I didn't do something so incredibly stupid that I've driven her away forever.

It does occur to me that this thought process is a little ridiculous.

I mean really, who is Frankie? Will I ever see her again after this vacation? Most likely no. Why would I? She'll stay here and continue her job, and I'll fly home and be alone in my townhouse. But right now, on this day, in this moment, I have the unstoppable urge to find her. Maybe piece together some of what happened last night, if it's not too humiliating.

Maybe kiss her again.

An African-American lesbian couple is at a table across the restaurant, but even from where I'm sitting, they are adorable and in love. Beneath the table, their sandaled feet are touching. Above the table, they're holding hands. They've barely looked around the restaurant; they seem only to have eyes for each other. I am happy for them, but I feel my heart crack in my chest just a little because I am also envious. I want that. I *so* want that. I want somebody who knows me like the back of her hand, somebody who knows exactly how I like my coffee and will bring it to me each morning. Somebody who is first and foremost in my mind at all times, and vice-versa. Somebody who is the first person I want to see in the morning and the last person I want to see before I go to sleep. Somebody I can take care of. Somebody who will take care of me.

I blink hard and pull my gaze away.

I sign the tab with my room number, gather my things, and head out of the restaurant, donning my sunglasses the second I come remotely close to a beam of sunshine. The ibuprofen isn't helping all that much, and I begin reciting the internal monologue that every hung over person gets to eventually. *You are an idiot. You did this to yourself. You're lucky all you have is a hangover. Let's hope no incriminating photos or videos show up on YouTube.* That kind of thing.

I cross the ornate lobby, struck by the influx of people. Then I remember it's Saturday, and it's probably their biggest check-in day. It's the day Kim and I were due to check in as a married couple. I wonder how many of the men and women mingling around the registration desk are here on their honeymoons, how many of them I'll run into in my hallway on my way back to my room.

I grimace and take a quick detour toward the pool. Maybe hanging with Allison will help my mood.

The weather is gorgeous—sunny, electric blue sky, eighty-five degrees—and it immediately aggravates me. Why should it be so perfect outside when I feel so gloomy inside? Stupid Florida weather. It occurs to me then that Christmas is in three days. Well, four if you count today. But I want today to be over already, so I'm not counting it. Christmas is in three days as far as I'm concerned. Sunday, Monday, Tuesday, and then Christmas. I should give my mother a call, but I'm surprised to note that not only don't I have my phone with me, but I haven't even checked in since Kim's unfeeling text yesterday. I feel completely disconnected from my life, and I'm honestly not sure if that is something that I am enjoying or freaking out about. A little of both, I think.

The pool deck is very busy. I realize that I didn't check with Allison about *which* pool she'd be at, but I have to assume it's this one, the only one we've visited. I stand just inside the entryway and scan the crowd. It's got to be double what it's been the past two times we were here, but it's a good-sized space, and though the crowd is thicker, it doesn't feel like it's overpopulated.

Two young, tanned men run past me in Speedos, then jump into the pool—something I'm reasonably sure they're not supposed to do—and I get hit with a few drops. I shift my stance and move a bit to my left, and then I can see Allison. Her dark hair is shining in the sun, her big sunglasses masking her eyes. She's got a book in her hand, but she's holding it face down on her thigh because she's having a conversation with the young Athletic Cutie from our first day here. Again clad in board shorts and a short-sleeve, tight-fitting swim shirt, she's leaning close to Allison, rapt with attention. A small grin crosses my face. Most people look like that when Allison is talking.

I watch for a while. I don't want to interrupt. Allison has already told me this girl is too young, but she's adorable and obviously interested. Who doesn't love when somebody gives you every ounce of their attention? I'd eat it up. It's been too long.

There's an empty stool at the bar, and I feel like sitting, so I take it. The bartender sets a pair of rum runners up on the surface for a customer, and the mere sight of them makes the eggs and bacon digesting in my stomach threaten to make a reappearance. I swallow hard, glad when a hair-covered gentleman walks away with them.

"What can I get you?" the bartender asks me.

"Just a Diet Coke. Please."

I sit and watch for a few minutes, sipping my soda, feeling its bubbles help settle my stomach. Allison is still talking to Athletic Cutie, and I wonder what they could be discussing. Though Allison is pretty well-versed in a wide variety of subjects. I think about what she and Athletic Cutie might have in common. Music? It's possible. Allison's tastes range far and wide, from today's hip-hop to old Motown, and 70s Chicago. Movies? Could be, though Allison tends to lean toward independent films rather than the big-budget blockbusters Athletic Cutie probably likes. I picture her waiting in line at midnight for tickets to the next installment of *Transformers*. Sports? That's likely. Allison loves the WNBA. She's been to dozens of games. She follows golf (which puts me to sleep in, like, five seconds flat). She loves football, and has even been known to catch a baseball game or two (even though she thinks they run *way* too long). Athletic Cutie laughs, a deep hearty laugh that makes me smile when I hear it, and sets her hand on Allison's thigh. I look away.

"Hey, you."

The woman next to me is smiling, approachable. She's got reddish-brown hair pulled back in a ponytail, big blue eyes, and a small dimple on her left cheek. I have no idea who she is.

"Hi," I say in reply.

"You don't remember me, do you?"

Oh, god. I swallow hard, wet my lips, sip my Diet Coke, absolutely no idea what to say.

"It's okay," she says, and her voice and manner are good-natured, so I'm slightly relieved. "I told you last night you probably wouldn't."

I can feel my face flush, and I slowly shake my head back and forth as I close my eyes.

She laughs, puts a gentle hand on my shoulder and squeezes. "Hey, it's okay. It's fine. You had a few rum runners and were feeling no pain. I know that. Hell, you said that."

"I said that?" I am mortified. Exactly what I hoped wouldn't happen is happening. My alcohol-infused evening is coming back to bite me squarely in the ass.

"Those exact words, I'm pretty sure."

"Oh, god. I'm so sorry. Whatever I did, whatever I said, I am so, so sorry."

She laughs again, orders a gin and tonic from the bartender. "No apologies necessary. You were charming. We danced."

"We danced?"

"We did. You were very good."

I frantically search my memory banks, surreptitiously looking at the woman, trying to find any flash of her whatsoever, but I fail. I shake my head again.

"It's okay," she says again, but gentler this time. "We just danced." She sips her drink. "You only had eyes for the Mistletoe Dyke."

I choke on my Diet Coke. "I'm sorry. What?"

"That's what everybody was calling her. The Mistletoe Dyke. She carried around a sprig of mistletoe and used it to kiss as many women as possible. Kind of ingenious, really. Wish I'd thought of it."

Is she talking about Frankie?

Instantly, my brain tosses me an image of Frankie pulling a piece of mistletoe from her vest, holding it over my head, and kissing me senseless.

Yup.

I nod my head. I don't like the implication that Frankie was using mistletoe on more than just me, but I'm nearly ecstatic to have an actual memory from the previous night. It gives me hope that more will return to me as the day wears on.

"I'm Jessica, by the way," the ponytailed woman says, and holds out her hand.

"Mackenzie," I say, and shake.

"Oh, I know."

I glance at her, but she doesn't elaborate. I squint a little bit. "We just danced, right?"

"I promise. We just danced. I would have done more..." She lets the sentence dangle, picks up her drink, then says, "Thanks for the dances, Mackenzie. Let me know if you give up the Mistletoe

Dyke and want to try something more...stable." With a wink, she leaves me sitting at the bar with what I'm sure is a bewildered expression on my face.

The bartender refills my Diet Coke without asking. I like that, and I nod my thanks. Spinning in my chair so I can see the pool again, I scan and see that Athletic Cutie is still chatting up Allison. I contemplate a rescue, but Allison seems to be enjoying herself, so instead, I people-watch.

Over in the corner of the pool, I see Spikey Blonde from our first elevator ride on our first day, the one who was drunk and hitting on Allison. I find it interesting that in a resort so enormous, I keep seeing the same handful of people. Spikey Blonde is still with the same redhead and a couple others, but they seem sober and relaxed today, lounging in the sun, talking quietly to one another. I flash back to her stumbling flirtation with Allison in the elevator, and I wonder how close to that behavior I might have been last night. And do I really want to know? I just met a woman that I apparently danced with more than once, and yet I don't have a sliver of recognition in my head. That frightens me.

The music on the sound system changes to Lady Gaga's *Bad Romance*, and as if on cue, I get a flash of dancing with Jessica. We danced to this song. We danced close. I mean *close*. Like, dirty dancing. I cover my eyes with my hand.

"Jesus Christ," I mutter, the sickening feeling that I'd made an absolute spectacle of myself starting to seep in.

"One of those days?" the bartender asks. He's very handsome, very tan, and has kind brown eyes.

"One of those months," I respond.

"Want something stronger in the Diet Coke?"

"I do, but I'm going to pass. But thank you."

"Sure thing." He goes off to help another customer.

I notice that Athletic Cutie has left Allison to her own devices. Finally. I scoop up my Diet Coke and head her way. I lean close to her and tug the ear bud out of one ear.

"Hey, what did the Polish mother say when her daughter told her she was pregnant?"

Allison shakes her head. "No idea. What?"

"Are you sure it's yours?"

Allison snorts a laugh. "That's a good one."

I sit on the end of her lounge by her feet.

She gestures to my cup with her chin. "Rum?"

I shoot her a look. "Coke."

"Smart."

"Every once in a great while, it does happen."

We sit quietly, watching the people, soaking in the sun.

"I saw your little puppy dog drooling on you again," I say, hoping my voice doesn't sound to her as sarcastic as it does to me.

"She's cute. Her name's Shelly. She's here with her buds. Three of them. They're all teachers and have been saving all year for this trip."

"Well, she certainly likes you."

I can feel Allison's eyes on me, but she doesn't say anything. I decide it's a good time to change the subject. "Three days until Christmas."

"Yup."

"I should probably call my mother."

"That's a good idea. I think there are a couple missed calls on your phone."

Again, it occurs to me how out of touch I've been the past couple days. I kind of like it. Don't get me wrong. I love my cell phone. I love texting. I love being able to get online with my phone. At the same time, it's hard to be available always. I guess technology has pros and cons. I recall reading an article about working mothers and how the invention of the cell phone had been hardest on them. Now, not only can they not escape their bosses, they can't escape their children either. They've become constantly accessible. Sometimes, I feel that way with my mother. It's harder to avoid somebody's call if they know that their number shows up on your phone and that your phone basically says, *Hey! You missed this call!*

"I miss the days when I could claim my answering machine tape had run out."

A chuckle bubbles up from Allison's chest as she puts her earbuds back in. I stand up and take my leave, but she closes a warm hand on my wrist. "Hey, can you do me a favor?"

"Sure."

"Can you get me a rum runner before you leave?"

I stare at her for a moment, but I can't see her eyes due to her sunglasses, so I'm not sure if she's messing with me. I nod and she lets me go. I get the drink and hold it as far away from my nose as I can, keeping my arm straight out in front of me as I walk it back to her, grimacing the entire time.

She thanks me, takes it, and leans back in her chair, savoring the first sip like a parched woman in the desert. I glare at her for a few seconds, but she seems not to notice.

My room is peaceful, and I briefly entertain the idea of just staying in it for the remainder of my vacation. When I open the sliding glass door, the ocean breeze enters like a welcome visitor, gently rearranging my hair and ruffling the sheer panels. I inhale deeply and wonder what it is about the salt air that makes one feel suddenly calm and relaxed. I've never been one of those people who has the inexplicable desire to live by the water. I'm happy in my northeastern home of lush trees, green grass, and white Christmases. But even I have to admit there's something amazing about the sound of the surf and the smell of the ocean.

I grab my phone and a bottle of water and take a seat out on the balcony. Again, I sit and breathe, avoiding having to deal with anything other than taking in air, letting air out. After a few moments, I feel calm, so I turn on the phone to see what awaits me.

Five texts.

Three missed calls.

I sigh and hit the texts first. Two more from Kim, one from last night, one from this morning. The first one is along the same lines as the one from earlier.

Hope ur ok 2day. Ur on my mind. I hate that she uses text speak like she's in high school. She's almost forty. She can't spell out the word 'you're'?

The second one is a bit more surprising.

Can we talk sometime? I miss u. I don't like that. I have nothing to say to her. Do I? Well, I can probably come up with a few choice things to say to her, but none of it would be kind, pleasant, or anything she'd want to hear. I click to the next text, deciding I'll deal with Kim later.

Where are you? This one is from Allison, as are the next two. I furrow my brow and check the times. Last night when I was in the club. I think. Ugh. I delete them and move on to the missed calls.

One is from my mother. She left a message. One is from the office at home. They also left a message. The third is from Allison's number, but no message, again from last night.

I punch in my codes and listen to the voicemail messages. The one from work is no big deal. My boss just checking to see how I'm doing, tell me she was thinking about me yesterday. That's nice. I make a mental note to send her a text and say thanks.

My mom's message makes me smile.

"Hi, honey. It's Mom." I love how she always identifies herself when she leaves me a message, as if I haven't heard that voice for thirty-five years and couldn't possibly guess who it is. "I just wanted to say hi, see how you're doing down there. I know this is a hard day for you, but you remember that if that stupid girl doesn't want to be with you, she's…well, she's just stupid. Any woman would be lucky to have you. So, have a cocktail—but not too many—and try to just enjoy yourself. Give me a call if you get a chance. Christmas isn't the same without you here. Love you, honey."

Unexpectedly, my eyes well up. My mom can be pushy, nosy, and downright irritating, but she loves me and never in my life have I ever doubted that. No way would she let me.

I take a big slug from the water bottle, then hit Mom's number.

"Merry Christmas. Campbell residence." This is how she answers the phone from December 1 through the day after Christmas. I can hear Christmas music in the background, and I can almost swear I smell cookies in the oven.

"Hey, Mom."

"Mackenzie? Oh, hi, sweetie! How are you? How is Allison? Are you all right? I was just thinking about you." I swipe at my cheek with the back of my hand.

"I'm good. We're fine. It's beautiful here. You'd love it. Our room has a balcony overlooking the ocean. We're on the twentieth floor."

"Twentieth? My god. You be careful, Mackenzie. I read about all kinds of accidents. People fall off balconies all the time, you know."

I stifle a laugh. She doesn't like it when I laugh at her ridiculous warnings. They're not ridiculous to her. Me getting drunk and falling off the twentieth floor balcony is a totally possible occurrence in her mind. "I'll be careful, Ma. No falling for me. Promise."

"How's the weather?"

"Ridiculously gorgeous. Sunny. The sky is the color of a robin's egg every single day. It's about eighty, eighty-five. I almost feel guilty."

Mom laughs. "Well, we got four inches of snow last night, so don't feel too bad. It's not even going to get out of the twenties today."

"Are you making cookies?"

"Cut-outs. My second batch. The kids are coming over later to help decorate them." The kids refers to my brother Brad's son and daughter. It's a family tradition that they help Grandma decorate the cut-out cookies—usually the second batch because my father can't keep his hands off batch number one. I am typically there, too. My heart starts to ache a little bit as Mom continues. "And then I think I'll try a new recipe I found in a magazine. They're chocolate peppermint squares."

"They sound good. Festive."

"If they come out all right, I'll put some away for you. I already boxed up some of the thumbprint cookies and your Grandma gave me some fig cookies to freeze for you."

The ache thrums a little stronger. "Thanks, Mom," I say softly. I expected to miss my family while here, but it's suddenly a lot harder than I thought.

"Is Allison taking good care of you down there?"

"She is. We're having a nice time." I decide not to tell her about last night, my being over-served and making out with a virtual stranger who I have yet to find today.

"Good. She's a good girl, that Allison. I like her."

I grin. "She likes you, too, Mom."

We talk about a few more insignificant things, both of us knowing we're just trying to stay on the phone a bit longer, neither of us wanting to address the fact that I should really be home. It's Christmas. It's not the time to be away from family. But my mom surprises me every so often and actually leaves something alone that should be left alone. If she pressed too heavily on how much she misses me, how much she wishes I was home right now, it would be very hard for me to stay here, and she knows I need this away time. So she stays quiet, even though I know it's killing her. That's my mom.

"It's lunch time," she says once we've exhausted all other topics. "Have you had lunch? You should have some lunch."

"Good idea. There's a great little café downstairs."

"Oh, nice. I bet they have good sandwiches." My mom's a big proponent of the sandwich. She thinks they're practical.

"I bet they do, too. I'll go check."

"Okay. And make sure Allison eats too. That girl is too skinny."

I smile. "I will, Mom. Have fun with the kids tonight, okay? Give them hugs for me? And don't let them eat all the cookies."

We say our goodbyes, with me promising to call her again soon.

I hang up the phone, gaze out at the ocean, and decide I'm done wallowing for the moment. Time to go do something.

Chapter Thirteen

I KNOW I TOLD MY mother I'd eat some lunch, but breakfast wasn't that long ago, and frankly, my stomach still isn't in the best of shape. I feel okay, but I suspect putting the wrong thing into my digestive system could be catastrophic. As in, send me back to worship the porcelain god once again, this time while I'm fully aware. No, thanks.

I decide I should make an honest effort to find Frankie, rather than wandering around the resort on the off chance that I'll maybe bump into her.

Looking in the mirror is not a pleasant activity for me today, but it has to be done. At least the dark circles are easing up a bit. My hair's not bad; the past couple of days in the sun have really lightened it, brought out some gold highlights that I pay good money for at home in the winter. I touch up my makeup, spritz on a little perfume, change from gym shorts into slightly more presentable cargos, smooth my palms over my clothes. That's about as good as it's going to get.

I pocket my key card and phone and head out.

The Rainbow's Edge is buzzing as much now as it was earlier, people milling around, meeting for the first time, cuddling, kissing, holding hands, staring in awe at the high ceilings and ornate decorations of the lobby. The registration desk is still bustling with activity as I pass, the employees busy, but smiling.

They do a good job here.

The thought zips through my mind. It's so true. I have yet to come across a waiter, a bartender, or housekeeping staff that's been anything less than friendly and pleasant. Not an easy feat to accomplish for such a huge business.

I take my time as I wander, trying to focus in on the décor, the fancy crown molding, the burgundy and gold carpeting, the wide variety of artwork on the walls. As I walk, I do two things. I people-watch, which is a given, especially in a place where the majority of the occupants are gay. There's something about looking at a woman I think is attractive, but knowing that the chance that she's straight is a lot lower here than it is in any given situation at home that I find to be…exhilarating.

The other thing I do is think about the designer of this entire resort. The whole theme seems to be almost Greco-Roman and I wonder why. Is it because of all the sculptures of naked men and women, and so designing the buildings with a Greco-Roman theme was the best way to ensure that naked statues fit in? And then when the decision was made to go in that direction, they really had no choice but to use ivory, burgundy, and gold as the color scheme. Then they must have figured, "Well, hell. If we're going with the look of ancient Greece and Rome, we'd better throw in some pillars, a few fountains, and a lot of marble just to make sure it all blends." It seems like an odd choice for a resort on the beach, but I don't hate it. It is surprisingly not as tacky as it could be. That's not to say it isn't a little tacky, but it's okay. I kind of like it.

The massage suite is open, but Rob isn't on duty, and it occurs to me that, though this is a resort, a vacation spot for most people, for the employees, it's a job. And Rob probably works Monday through Friday. The man behind the counter today is no less handsome than Rob—blonde, very tan, with toned shoulders and just enough stubble on his face to be deemed sexy rather than messy. His nametag says he's Trey. Of course he is.

"Hi there," he says with a smile that reveals unsurprisingly perfect teeth and a tiny dimple high on his right cheek. I figure the boys must swoon over him, since I practically am. "Are you here for an appointment?"

"No." I lean on the counter with my forearms and lower my voice. "I'm looking for Frankie. Is she here today?"

An expression zips across his face so quickly I don't have time to identify it, and his smile dims just a watt or two. "No, I'm afraid she's not here today. It's her day off."

I inhale, blow it out slowly. "Do you know where I might find her?"

He's beginning to look decidedly uncomfortable when a door opens behind me and somebody else enters the room. I turn to see a tall, fit woman, her light brown hair pulled back from her face, tiny crow's feet pointing out from the corners of her blue eyes as she gives me a smile. I glance down and see the paw print socks on her feet and recognition is immediate.

"Stella?" I say.

Her light brows furrow. "Yes…" Her voice trails off.

I poke my chest with my forefinger. "Mackenzie Campbell. I was in here yesterday for a couple's massage with my friend?"

She nods. "Oh, right. Hi."

"She's looking for Frankie." Trey's tone has changed. It's still very friendly, but it's a bit harder than before. When I glance back at him, he's giving Stella a look that baffles me, but she apparently gets perfectly.

"I see."

Trey hands Stella a clipboard. She takes it, signs something, and hands it back just as the door opens and two men come in, smiling. I step back from the desk, making room for them and they proceed to check in with Trey. Taking a deep breath, Stella closes her hand gently but firmly on my elbow and steers me away from them toward a corner of the waiting area.

"Okay, look. I don't know what you got into with Frankie, but you should just let it go."

I'm sure my bewilderment is written all over my face because she looks at me and very nearly rolls her eyes.

"This is what she does. It's her MO. She finds a cute vacationer, charms her, maybe wines and dines her, spends the night. And most of the time? Breaks her heart." She shakes her head, and her eyes are troubled as she gazes off into the distance. "I've seen it too many times. Then they come looking for her, but she's conveniently disappeared and they're crushed."

I swallow hard, not sure what to make of this. "Um, I don't think anything happened last night. I mean, I had too much to drink..." My voice trails off as I recognize just how pitiful I probably sound to her.

Stella is nodding like she's heard it all before.

"I just wanted to find her to say thanks," I say, sounding completely lame even to my own ears.

"Thanks?" Stella's face says she's skeptical.

"Yes. She took care of me. Got me back to my room. Stayed with me while I got sick." I grimace. "Put me to bed."

"Put you to bed or took you to bed?" The sarcasm is clear and biting.

"Okay," I say, suddenly feeling the urge—no, the need—to leave, to get away from the judgment of Stella. I guess I can understand it. It sounds like Frankie's got a reputation for womanizing and maybe Stella worries that it interferes with business? I don't know. I don't care. I want out of this weird female pissing contest. "Thanks for your help." I turn to leave, but Stella has my elbow again. I turn to face her, but I really don't want to hear any more.

"Look. I'm sorry." Her voice is just above a whisper so only I can hear. "You seem like a nice woman. It's just that I've seen this too many times. You're actually in good shape compared to some of the girls who come in here the morning after. Crying. Devastated." She shakes her head. "Frankie's no good for you. She's really no good for anybody. Yes, she's charming, she's good-looking, she knows how to treat a lady. Until she gets what she wants. Then she's done. She's put her job in jeopardy more than once because she can't keep her hands to herself."

"Why are you telling me this?"

"I don't know." Stella lets go of my arm. "I don't know. I'm just...I guess I'm tired of seeing the carnage she leaves behind. Like I said, you seem like a nice girl. I don't want that to happen to you." She doesn't let me respond. She just gives me a sad smile and leaves me standing there. When I look back at Trey, his expression is similar.

These people think I'm pathetic.

That idea doesn't please me at all, but I'm at a loss for the moment, so I stand there probably looking the part as I contemplate my next move.

So, Frankie is a womanizer. Huh. That doesn't make a lot of sense to me. Yes, I was drunk, but I am reasonably sure I'd be able to tell if I'd had sex the previous night despite my intoxication. Right? I doubt Frankie would've hung around to do the dirty deed with somebody unconscious. Where's the satisfaction in that? And every woman has telltale signs her body tosses at her. My thighs don't ache. My lips aren't chapped. I recall nothing sexual beyond the kiss at the bar. No, I don't think we went all the way. What I do think is that Frankie took good care of me when I couldn't take care of myself. Despite what Stella says about her, that deserves my thanks.

There's a wing here, off on the east side of the resort, where all the employees are housed.

The line comes out of nowhere, hits my brain as if it'd just been broadcast over a loudspeaker. Immediately, I flash to asking Frankie where she lives. That was her answer. She lives here. On the premises. So even though it's her day off, she's still here. I wonder if she's up for visitors.

With a big grin and wave to Trey—who looks decidedly confused by my whiplash-inducing change in demeanor—I head for the door.

I don't think the staff is supposed to tell the customers where the employee housing is. I asked a couple of the housekeepers, but they either looked at me vaguely or pretended they didn't speak English. Frankie said the East Wing. I'm no geographer, but I'm pretty sure I can find east.

I head off in the direction the sun's been rising since I got here. This place is huge. I mean, I knew it was very large, but it's freaking enormous. I don't think I quite realized the scope of size a resort would need to house three thousand people at any given time. I feel like I've been walking for days, but I suspect that's because I'm still weak and drained from last night's reveling. I'm definitely moving slower than usual. My legs feel like somebody snuck into my room while I slept and poured a few pounds of sand into each one. My eyes are still kind of scratchy. My mouth tastes like something crawled inside and died. Still. I unwrap my fourth piece of gum today and start chewing.

Everybody here is so damned happy. I suppose that's good for business. I mean, who wants to vacation someplace where everybody walks around like me: miserable and hung over? I approach a group of men—there must be ten or twelve of them—all laughing and nudging playfully at one another. They pass me by in a cloud of cologne, which is usually way too much for me to deal with, but one of them is wearing something really nice… subtle and musky. I like it. Following them are two women signing to each other. I can pick out "eat" and "salty" from the brief ASL class I took in college, but that's all I get before they're past me.

I have also passed two more restaurants, another club, and one of the fitness centers—which is filled to capacity with sweating men in various styles of workout clothing. Running, biking, lifting. They're all very busy. I know gay men often have the reputation of focusing too heavily on their physical appearance, but judging from the men working out today, it's worth it. I stop to watch, and every last one of them that I can see through the glass wall has a gorgeous physique. I'm envious.

Kim used to work out like a fiend. Well, I imagine she still does. It always sort of mystified me. I don't enjoy exercising while standing in one place. I love to be outdoors. I love to hike (or just walk). I love to play catch or Frisbee or even do yard work. That's all exercise to me. Standing in the same room and lifting a heavy piece of steel up and down, up and down, up and down…snore. I can't imagine much that would bore me faster. But she was all about her workouts. She'd get up at five in the morning and drive her ass to the gym, even during a blizzard, just to make sure she didn't miss a workout. I suggested once that she should just buy what she needed and set up a home gym in our house. She said there was something about the atmosphere of the gym that helped her get a better workout than if she tried to exercise at home alone.

As I stand there and observe—and notice two women as well as the twenty-seven guys—I can almost understand what she meant. I guess if everybody around you is doing something to burn calories, you're more likely to want to keep up. I don't know. It looks incredibly tedious to me.

I watch for a few more minutes, then continue on my eastward trek.

Five more minutes of walking and I get to the gift shop. The Pot O' Gold. How creative for someplace called The Rainbow's Edge. Or not. It's pretty sizable, and I window shop for about ten and a half seconds before I decide to wander around inside. Why not?

The inventory makes me chuckle, and I think about how almost ADD you'd have to be to do the ordering for stock. There's a little bit of everything here, truly. First, the essentials of any hotel: toiletries, cosmetics, first aid. God forbid somebody goes on vacation and forgets to bring their toenail clippers. I did go on a business trip once and my luggage arrived at the hotel 24 hours later than I did; I was happy the hotel gift shop carried toothbrushes, that's for sure. Then, you've got your snack food. Because hotel guests get weird cravings, don't they? I pick up a bag, trying to remember the last time I got a hankering for pork rinds on a trip. Or ever. Everything from chips and crackers to chocolate truffles and Swedish fish stare back at me from the snack wall. A cooler houses sodas, beer, bottled water (a necessity in this state), and even a few brands of wine—surprisingly good ones.

I keep walking along and get to the books and magazines. How in the world do you decide what to keep in stock? You've got guests from all walks of life here, and maybe they want some reading material for while they sit by the pool. Books, I could probably manage to handle, but magazines? How do you decide—

not only between periodicals that are alarmingly similar (*Vogue, Cosmo, Marie Claire*), but between subject matter? How do you choose golf over fishing or cooking over sewing? I'd end up tearing my hair out.

Next, we get to the apparel. My favorite part of any gift shop. I love sweatshirts. I love T-shirts. I try to get one from any place I've ever been. The Rainbow's Edge is no exception; I fully plan on increasing my wardrobe by at least one piece by the time I leave here. I run my hands over the fleece pullovers (which seem oddly out of place in Florida), the resort logo subtly embroidered on the left chest. I like that. I don't like that it's $89, but I file it away in my mind and move on. Hooded sweatshirt. Always nice, but the logo is a bit too big and…rainbow-y. No, not that one. Long sleeve T-shirts. Love them. And there's a nice women's cut with a slimmer fit and a V-neck. I file that away as well. Crewneck sweatshirt is next.

This one would work for Kim; she doesn't like hoodies.

I stop, my hand grasping the shoulder of the crewneck, about to hold it up for evaluation. I blow out an irritated breath, hang it back on its rack, and walk my ass right out of the apparel section altogether, vowing to come back later. Or tomorrow. Or never.

The next section of the store is the gifty stuff. Shot glasses. Novelty pens. Pennants that say Florida on them. Picture frames. Little plastic flamingoes (what the hell do you do with those?). There's also a small shelf of holiday things. Tree ornaments. Snow globes. The ever-present Santa hats. I pick up a snow globe and shake it, remembering Allison's story, suddenly seeing the image of little Allison trying to shake all the snow globes on the shelf before the first one's snow has all fallen. It makes me smile.

With a sigh, I move on, buy myself a Snickers bar (for a ridiculous three dollars) to tamp down an unexpected sugar craving, and leave the shop, continuing on my way east.

A weird thought hits me as I walk, entertaining what a good *Twilight Zone* episode it would make if I just had to keep walking forever, moving endlessly east but never reaching my destination. It's starting to feel that way, and my feet ache. A combination of last night's dancing and spending three solid days in flip-flops, which give me no support whatsoever (but look cute). Then my non-stop internal monologue wanders into the territory that talks about how cool it would be to have a massage therapist as a partner because you could get really good foot rubs every day. Of course, if that's what she does for a living, rubbing her partner's feet would probably be the last thing she'd want to do at the end of the day. Still…

That train of thought chugs me into Frankie Station, and then I'm right back to the beginning, wondering if I will ever find Frankie, and if I do, what happens next? I'm seriously starting to marvel over the endlessness of The Rainbow's Edge when I see a glass door down the hall I'm traveling. It's closed and has a keypad next to it for unlocking. Black letters stenciled across the glass tell me it's the entrance to Employee Housing. Below that, it tells me that Authorized Only people can get in.

I tug the door handle anyway because who knows? The stenciling could be mistaken.

It's not.

How the hell do I get to Frankie now? I'm frustrated.

With sagging shoulders, I turn back toward the bank of elevators down the hall a bit and plop down on a cushioned bench situated there. I just need to think.

After a moment or two, I hear a click. The glass door opens down the hall and an older gentleman comes out. As he approaches my bench, I see he's dressed in a sort of tux and I surmise he must be heading to work at one of the restaurants. He smiles pleasantly at me, hits the Up button on the elevator, and waits. When it dings, he points to it and raises his eyebrows.

"Oh, no. I'm just...resting," I tell him. He nods, boards the elevator, and is gone.

I lean my head back against the wall and shut my eyes. Just breathe. The enormity of my situation feels heavy today. I was supposed to be married yesterday. It's a fact that I have recognized several dozen times throughout this trip, and I'm starting to get annoyed. This should have been my honeymoon. I shouldn't even be sitting here right now. I should be up in my Honeymoon Suite —a room that cost a *very* pretty penny—still in bed with my new wife because we can't get enough of each other. I should have sore thighs and swollen lips and I should be dehydrated from all the fluids I've lost during the fifteen orgasms I've had since our arrival. I should have all of that.

Instead, I'm sitting near the employee wing of the resort like some sort of inept stalker waiting for a woman who held my hair while I puked last night. God, I hope I didn't try to kiss her with my vomit mouth. I shake my head back and forth, mortified all over again that I acted like a college freshman last night.

"What a turn-on I must have been," I mutter to the empty hallway, opening my eyes as I reach the conclusion that this is a futile—and pathetic—course of action.

Just as I'm preparing to stand and walk the thirty-five miles of hallway back to the lobby, the employee door clicks, and I turn that way to look.

It's Frankie. And she's not alone.

Chapter Fourteen

FRANKIE SMILES WHEN SHE sees me, despite the fact that her arm is wrapped comfortably around the waist of an extremely pretty woman whose auburn hair looks like inviting warmth falling around her shoulders; for a brief moment, I want to bury my face in it.

I stand for their approach, and Frankie's smile never falters. It's not the smile of somebody who knows me, though. It's a polite smile. She's wearing khaki cargo shorts and a tight black T-shirt that hugs her strong shoulders. Her hair is freshly styled—I can smell the hair gel—and the spikes in the front are adorable. Tevas adorn her feet, and a tattoo I never noticed before encircles her left calf. She smells terrific. Or maybe that's the auburn-haired woman. I don't care which one it is, I have to make a conscious effort not to inhale loudly.

"Hi there," Frankie says as the two of them pass me, and she pushes the Up button for the elevator.

"Hi, Frankie," I say. That gets her attention, the fact that I know her name, and when she turns back to me, I swear to god, she makes a subtly squinty face of puzzlement. Recognition hits her face then; I can see exactly when it happens. Recognition followed by caution.

"Oh, hey." The smile wattage dims only slightly. *She's good*, I think. Everything Stella said comes rushing into my head like a racing track team, and I grit my teeth together to keep from growling over her being right.

Well, I came to accomplish a certain task, and goddamnit, I'm going to do that. I take a breath, lick my lips, and dive in. "Listen,

Frankie, I know I wasn't the best company last night, but…" I trail off, searching for words. Frankie looks decidedly uncomfortable and shifts her weight. The auburn-haired woman's warmth is quickly evaporating. "I just wanted to say thanks. What you did for me, I really appreciate it."

Frankie blinks those blue eyes at me as if waiting for me to continue. When I don't, she gives her head one nod and says, "Oh. Okay. Sure."

"Thank you. Really."

Another one-nod nod. "You're welcome. Sure."

The elevator dings announcing its arrival, and I think, *Saved by the bell*, as Frankie and her date board as fast as they can without actually leaping onto it. Neither of them waits to see if I'm boarding too. Frankie doesn't look at me again. The auburn-haired woman's facial expression is alarmingly similar to the ones both Stella and Rob gave me at the massage studio. Pity. The doors slide shut, and I stand there, bewildered. And a little bit angry.

"What the hell was that?" I ask nobody. I actually sit back down on the bench and say, "Seriously? What *was* that?" Luckily, there's no one in the hallway to worry about (or report to upper management) the poor guest who's sitting alone and talking to herself.

I don't know how much time goes by before I finally drag my ass off the bench and start walking back the way I came. There's a lot going on inside me right now. Annoyance. Irritation. Hurt. Anger. Embarrassment. Yeah, embarrassment is a big one. I mean, let's be honest, I wasn't the one with the hokey clipping of mistletoe snuggled coincidentally in my pocket. *That* is embarrassing. Yes, I thought it was adorable at the time. I admit it. I was charmed. I can actually picture Stella's face in my head, shaking hers back and forth, that same expression of pity on her face.

Poor Mackenzie. She's so naïve and vulnerable since her girlfriend left her.

A mix of sadness and ire hits me as her voice echoes through my head. Come on, it hasn't been that long. My girlfriend left me a couple weeks ago. Aren't I allowed to be naïve and vulnerable for a little bit? Just a little? A few days? A couple hours? Why is it so bad that I soaked up the attention I was given by a sexy, charming woman? Why should *I* be the one who's embarrassed? I didn't do anything wrong. I drank too much, yes. I know that. It happens. But am I not allowed any slack at all for my situation? None?

I shake my head as I walk, just aggravated by the whole thing. I absently wonder if Ms. Auburn Hair was also a massage client. Would that be me on Frankie's arm today if the rum runners hadn't kicked my ass last night? Did she leave me and head right out to find her next victim? When did she find her? Did she even stay with me last night? Maybe she didn't. Maybe I'm all screwed up in my assumptions. Maybe she put me to bed and skedaddled as fast as she could after that.

After a bit of walking, it starts to look like I'm entering civilization again. People are milling about in various states of summer attire. Everything from jeans to bikinis to Speedos have made an appearance in the past five minutes I've been walking. I actually turn my head to follow a ripped young man in a Speedo and flip-flops as he passes me. I only disapprove of his state of undress for a quick second before it occurs to me that if I looked like him, I'd parade around almost naked, too.

I pull my phone out and shoot a quick text to Allison.

Where are you?

She hits me back a few seconds later.

Bar.

Well, that narrows things right down, doesn't it? With a sigh I ask her which one.

Happy Hour. South of the lobby.

I have no idea if that's the name of the bar or if she's simply celebrating Happy Hour. My phone tells me it's mid-afternoon, so that certainly could be it. But we haven't been on the south end yet, so I suspect this is also a new bar. Good. I need to talk this through with her because it's all driving me a little crazy.

It takes me nearly another fifteen minutes to find The Happy Hour Bar. It's cute. Dark when you first walk in, but then the entire outer wall opens up to let in the fresh sea air, the view of the ocean, stunning. Allison is sitting at the bar with her back to me. She is alone, and I release a relieved breath. I don't really want to spill my guts with her new friends nearby.

"Hey." I grab the stool next to her. "Did you hear about the 747 that crashed in a cemetery in Poland?"

"No," she says, her eyes glued to the golf match that's on the television. She sips from her glass.

"So far, Polish officials have recovered 2,000 bodies."

Allison snorts a laugh.

"Whatcha drinkin'?" I ask.

"Rum runner."

Just hearing the name of it makes me queasy. "You're killing me. You know that, right?"

A corner of her mouth lifts up in a half-grin. "But they're so good."

"Yes, they are. They also bite."

"Only if you drink fifteen of them." She turns to me and winks.

"Funny." The bartender approaches me then. She's a very tall brunette with close cropped hair, a leather vest that shows plenty of cleavage, and a glimmering nose ring.

"What can I get you?" she asks me with a friendly smile.

I throw caution to the wind. "A gin and tonic, please?"

"You got it."

Allison turns to look at me, her expression surprised. "I know, I know," I say. "Don't judge me."

She chuckles. "You're on vacation. No judgment here."

My drink arrives, and it's good. I take very small sips, vowing to pace myself. Gin is no kinder than rum if you don't respect it. I settle in and try to focus on the most boring sport known to mankind. At the commercial break, I speak.

"I talked to my mom this morning."

"Yeah? How is she?" Allison and my mother have always gotten along great.

"Good. She misses me. This is hard for her."

"I bet. Is it the first time you haven't been home for Christmas?"

I nod. "She didn't say anything, so I've got to give her credit. She hates not having her family all together over the holidays. It's killing her, but she never said a word. I can't believe she's being so good to me."

"Why not?" Allison looks at me with those blue eyes. "She loves you."

"Yeah." Allison's gaze feels kind of intense, but I can't pinpoint why. Instead, I change the subject. "Where are your new friends?"

"They had some kind of excursion today." She turns back to golf.

"Like swimming with dolphins or something?"

"Parasailing."

"Ah." That explains why she didn't join them. Allison is deathly afraid of heights. We sit quietly for several moments. When Allison signals the bartender for a refill, I speak again. "I found Frankie."

Allison nods. "Yeah?"

"Yeah. It was…odd."

"How so?"

My eyebrows meet just above my nose as I try to verbalize the scene from earlier. "She came out of the employee wing—"

"You went to the employee wing to look for her?" Allison interrupts. At my nod, she just shakes her head.

"What?"

"Nothing. Go on. You went to the employee wing and?"

I narrow my eyes at her, then continue. "I waited outside the door to the wing—it's locked—and when she finally came out, she had a woman with her."

Allison looks at me. "Well, that's not really a shock, is it?"

I grimace. "I guess not."

"What happened next?"

"I stopped her and told her I wanted to thank her. For last night. I'm not sure she even remembered me at first."

"Interesting."

"Then she was nice, accepted my thanks, but was…odd."

"How do you mean? What did you think would happen?" Allison's voice is a little softer now.

I throw up my hands. "Oh, hell. I don't know. I thought she'd actually remember me, that's for damn sure. I guess I didn't make as solid an impression as I thought. Which is probably a good thing considering how drunk I was."

Allison splutters a laugh. "You were *so* drunk."

"Jesus, I can't remember the last time that happened."

"July Fourth, three years ago," she says.

The memory hits me out of nowhere, and I make a sound very much like a bark. "Oh, my god, I forgot about that."

"Jell-O shots are not your friends." She grins at me.

"They are *so* not," I agree, recalling the party on the lake with about twenty-five other people. I was there with Kim, but we weren't an item yet. Allison was there with Marianne. Lots of other friends from various walks of life came and went, but the Jell-O shots were delicious. And deadly. Kim ended up tucking me into the back seat of the car before the fireworks even went off. "Thank god I wait for years between benders, huh?"

Allison gestures to my nearly empty cup. "You want another?"

"Water," I tell the bartender as she appears as if by telepathy.

"Smart," Allison says with a wink.

We sit in silence for a little while, but I finally have to speak up. "How can you watch this? Are you sleeping with your eyes open? Because I am."

Allison's shoulders move as she chuckles. "This sport takes great concentration. Enormous precision."

"This is *not* a sport."

Allison just grins and shakes her head. We've had this argument dozens of times. "You've never played, have you?"

"No."

"Then you are not allowed to judge how much athletic prowess it does or does not take."

"Does not."

We grin at each other, and I bump her with my shoulder. She turns back to the golf while I silently wonder how I'd get through all of this without Allie.

The crowd starts to grow as we sit companionably. A group of guys commandeer one corner of the bar, and they're loud, but not obnoxiously so. The group of young women at the table behind us are. I'm trying to give them a subtle look of "could you please keep it down just a bit?" when Allison's cell dings. She checks it, taps off a reply.

"The parasailers?" I ask.

"Yup. They want to meet up for dinner in an hour."

"Cool."

"You should come." She looks at me, her expression gentle. My instinct is to politely decline, but what else am I going to do? Eat by myself? I've done that all day. I'd rather be with people.

"You're sure? I won't be intruding?"

Allison's face brightens, and her surprise isn't completely hidden. She thought I'd say no. "Not at all."

"As long as it's okay with everybody."

"It's fine. You can be my date."

"How will Jules feel about that?" I ask, winking to take out any sting.

"You're ridiculous, Kenz," she replies, poking me with a finger.

The Reef is the fanciest of the restaurants, bars, and cafes we've patronized so far during our visit. It's dark and elegant, the décor all deep mahogany and brass accents. The tables are candle-lit, with white linen tablecloths and extravagant place settings, each containing more forks than I use in an entire day of meals.

Allison and I are each wearing the one dressy outfit we brought because we vowed we'd do at least one really nice dinner while we're here. I'm in my all-purpose little black dress, a simple number with capped sleeves and a v-neck. It's not necessarily chic, but it's smart. A silk scarf in black and silver, along with dangling silver earrings and some silver bangle bracelets, and it's suddenly perfectly appropriate for a nice restaurant. Allison is, as usual, stunning in a great pair of black slacks, a lavender button-down blouse, and a black vest. She looks fabulously sophisticated, and I take a minute just to look at her. Large gold hoop earrings and a touch of purple eye shadow top off the look. My slight heels would put me at a height advantage if she weren't also wearing slight heels. We stand eye-to-eye, and she gives me a wink. The dim lighting somehow accentuates the cleft in her chin, and it occurs to me that I will most likely have the hottest date in the room. I feel strangely honored to be with her.

"Ready?" she asks me.

"Ready."

Though I didn't expect our one fancy dinner would be with three other people, it's okay. I'm actually in a really good mood and looking forward to conversing with new acquaintances. I follow Allison to a table in the back along the windows. The sun is making its descent toward the horizon, the windows are open, and that ever-present salty breeze wafts around us like gentle fingertips. It's a gorgeous evening.

"Hey there," Allison says to her new friends.

They're all smiles and open, friendly expressions. Allison introduces me to Jess, a large woman with short red hair and black-framed glasses, who stands up and shakes my hand. Next is Amy, rather plain with short, curly brown hair and eyes that crinkle to slits when she smiles. She shakes my hand as well.

"And you remember Jules."

"Hey, Kenzie. Glad you could join us." Jules's smile is genuine, and despite any reservations I may have had about her initially, she seems happy to have us join them.

We sit, Jules to Allison's left, me to her right, Jess to my right, and the waiter hands us menus; the others already have theirs. Jess is scanning the wine list. "We were thinking of ordering a couple bottles of wine. You guys into that?"

Allison and I look at each other and nod, and I make a mental note to match any glass of wine with a glass of water. I do not relish the idea of a repeat performance of last night.

Some of us want white and some want red, so after what feels (and probably sounds) like a life and death debate, we decide on a bottle of Malbec and a bottle of Sauvignon Blanc. As we settle in to peruse the dinner menus, Allison says, "So? How was the parasailing?"

"Oh. My god." Jules puts down her menu and just looks at her friends. "It was unbelievable."

"It so was," Jess pipes in. "The weather was gorgeous. The water was beautiful. The wind was gentle."

"The view," Amy adds, then closes her eyes as if savoring the memory. "Stunning. You're up so high, but you feel…untethered. Like you're flying. It's incredible."

"It really is," Jules says and bumps Allison with her shoulder. "You should give it a try. We might go again tomorrow."

"Allison's afraid of heights," I tell her.

"You are?" Jules asks, turning to Allison for confirmation.

Allison shrugs. "Yeah. Always have been, ever since I was a kid."

"That's too bad."

"But you're okay on an airplane?" Amy asks.

"As long as I'm not in a window seat," Allison says with a grin.

The waiter arrives with our wine, opens both bottles, and gives Jess and Amy sips for approval. They nod, he pours, and soon we all have a glass. I go with the white. Allison opts for red.

"Well, it is too bad about the heights thing," Jess says, returning us to the subject. She turns to me. "What about you, Kenzie? Would you parasail?"

I press my lips together and really think about it. "I don't know. I'm not afraid of heights, but…that's a long way up, and there's not a whole lot holding you…" I let my voice trail off. "Probably not. I'm kind of a baby."

"Ain't that the truth," Allison says, not looking up from her menu, and I swat playfully at her.

"God, everything looks so good," Jules comments. "I'm having trouble deciding."

"Me, too." Jess taps my menu. "That strawberry kiwi salad sounds yummy."

"Mackenzie's allergic to kiwi," Allison says.

"Yeah? So's my niece," Jess tells us. She reaches for her pocket.

"Oh, no," Amy says with a quirk of her lips. "Now you've done it."

"Shut up," Jess tells her, then holds up her phone to show us a picture of a sweet little girl who looks to be about four. Her hair is as red as Jess's (my mom would call her a carrot-top), and she's got a road map of freckles on each cheek.

"Oh, my god," I say. "How do you not just eat her up?"

"It's hard," Jess tells us. "She can get anything she wants from Aunt Jess."

"And she knows it," says Amy.

Jess scrolls us through a dozen more photographs, but I don't mind. The pride in her smile is touching, and the kid is freaking adorable. The waiter interrupts to take our order, and Amy mutters a "thank god" that earns her a lively slap from Jess.

For the remainder of our dinner, we laugh, eat, joke, and simply enjoy each other's company. They're a fun trio, I have to admit it. Jess is a graphic designer, so she and Allison get stuck on some technical mumbo-jumbo that makes the rest of our eyes glaze over...a fact we're sure to tell them. Several times. Amy's partner is in the service and stationed overseas. This trip was a big decision for her because she didn't want to come without her, but her partner insisted she come and have a good time.

"When will she be home next?" I ask.

"Not sure," Amy tells me, more matter-of-factly than I think I'd be able to. "Possibly by next summer. Fingers crossed." She holds hers up.

"Wow. That's...amazing. I don't know how she does it. I don't know how *you* do it."

Amy shrugs and sips her wine. "It's in her blood. That's what she tells me. She's from a military family, and it's all she's ever wanted to do: serve her country."

"The world could use more people like her," Allison says.

"Hear, hear." Jess holds up her glass and we all follow suit, toasting to the US Military.

"What about you guys?" Amy asks. "You're both single?"

Allison and I nod.

"For how long?" Jules asks.

"A little over a year," Allison says.

"For about ten days," I say, shoveling a forkful of salmon into my mouth. The table goes silent, and I can't help but laugh.

"Ten days? Seriously?" Amy asks.

"Yup. This was supposed to be my honeymoon." I'm surprised at how easily I say it. Surprised and relieved. I don't have that stabbing pain that's been shooting through my heart every time I bring it up. Thank god. I sip my wine, feeling almost...free for the first time since my arrival. The table's occupants—with the exception of Allison—are all staring at me. "You guys. It's fine. It's okay. Allison's here with me. I'm having fun. Look." I gesture around the table. "I've made new friends. I'm good."

They look unconvinced, but gradually turn their attention back to their plates. When my eyes meet Allison's, she's smiling at me. I smile back, then eat some more.

"Well. That sucks," Jules says. "I'm sorry."

"Me, too," chime in both other women.

"Thanks," I say.

"What happened to your relationship, Allison?" Jess asks. "Were you guys together long?"

"A couple years," Allison says. "We just…didn't work anymore."

I've never known exactly what happened between Allison and Marianne. She's never gone into detail with me, except to say exactly what she just said to our new friends: that they didn't work anymore. I wonder what happened that's so bad she doesn't want to talk about it, even to me.

"And you guys?" Allison asks, looking first at Jess, then at Jules. "Jules, I know you're single, but since when?"

Jules makes a thinking face, then looks to Jess for confirmation. "What? Three years?"

Jess nods. "About that."

"Yeah," Jules continues. "We weren't great together, and once she left, I realized I kind of like being on my own. You know? I answer to nobody but me."

"And your dog," Jess adds.

"True. Betty Lou *is* my one true love."

"I'm sort of…dating," Jess tells us, then her face turns nearly as red as her hair, and we rib her about her blushing.

"That's great," Allison says. "Good for you."

"Yeah. It's cool. We actually met online. We live about 45 minutes apart, so we see each other once or twice a week so far. It's going well."

"That's awesome," I say. "It's funny how the stigma of online dating has changed." When nods go around the table like the girls are doing the wave at a football game, I go on. "It used to be something people hid or said quickly and quietly out of the side of their mouth. Now, I know probably four or five couples who've met that way. It's kind of amazing how fast it's all changed."

"It's really something," Jess says. "There are so many dating sites, but most of them are pretty cool. The questions are smart and intricate and they really do a good job matching you with similar people."

"How long did you chat online before you sent pictures to each other?" I ask. "That would be the nerve-wracking part for me. Okay, I really like this person, and I think she really likes me. What if she's totally unattractive to me? Or worse, what if I'm totally unattractive to her?"

Jess is nodding the whole time I'm talking, and when I finish, she jumps right in. "That happens. Happened to me twice."

"Ugh," I say.

"Damn right. Totally depressing." She shrugs and sips her wine. "But, then I met Carly, so I guess things happened the way they were supposed to."

She has such a glow of happiness and contentment about her that for a quick zip of a second, I am flooded with envy. Luckily, that feeling passes very quickly, and I decide simply that I'm happy for her. Just because I don't have the fairytale doesn't mean nobody else should have it either. Right?

We finish eating, and I'm pleasantly surprised to realize that I'm having a really great time. Lots of laughing and great stories.

These are nice women, and I find myself wishing they lived closer to Allison and me. Of course, if that were the case, Allison and Jules would most likely hook up. For some reason, I can't get a handle on how I'd feel about that. It would probably be good for Allison; she's been single too long. But then I'd have to share her. I realize this is the thought process of a twelve-year-old, but I can't help it. I've had Allison all to myself since she broke up with Marianne. Sharing her would be quite an adjustment for me.

"You guys up for some dancing?" Amy does a little sashay of her hips as we leave the restaurant, making us all laugh.

"Not if that's what you call dancing," Jules teases her. "You'll embarrass us."

Amy smacks her. "Bitch. Come on, you guys. I feel like dancing." She then launches into her own rendition of *You Make Me Feel like Dancing*, complete with falsetto. The rest of us crack up.

"Yes," Jess says. "That totally convinces me that I want to be seen with you in a public place."

Allison turns to me. "What do you think? You up for it?"

I am. I really am. But I feel a weird need for a little alone time, something I haven't really allowed myself to absorb without my mind racing in a million directions. "I'm up for it," I say. Then I add, "But I think I'm going to walk off some of my dinner first. Can I meet up with you in, say, half an hour or so?"

Allison ducks her head a little to catch my eye. I look back at her, let her see me. When she's convinced I'm fine, that I'm not bailing, she gives me a subtle nod. "Do you want me to come with you?"

"No, I'm fine. Really. I just need to decompress a little bit. I'll catch up."

"You're sure?" Jess asks. "Don't make me come looking for you." She winks at me.

"I promise. A quick walk on the beach and I'll find you guys. You going to Night Moves?"

"God, that name sucks," Jules mutters, and I laugh.

"It does *not* suck," Amy protests. "It's awesome." I think she's a little drunk.

"That's because you are a child of the seventies," Jess says.

"The seventies were awesome," Amy says with determination.

Jess hooks an arm in Amy's. "Okay, Donna Summer. Let's go dance the night away." She leads her in the direction of the club, and the rest of us chuckle as we hear Amy wailing her grief over how hideously unjust it is that Donna Summer is dead.

Allison turns to me, raises a questioning eyebrow.

I lay my hand on her arm, notice its firmness under my fingers, tighten my grip just a tad. "I'm fine. I promise. A little sand beneath my feet and I'll meet up with you guys. I swear."

"Okay. I'll keep an eye out." Allison gives me that smile, and then she and Jules follow the path Amy and Jess took. I watch them go.

I wander through the resort to the nearest exit facing the beach and push my way through the glass double doors. The weather here is ridiculous. It really is. Sunshine, blue skies, ocean breeze. It's like a postcard...which would be fine if it wasn't like this every minute of every day. The fact that it never changes is almost eerie, like I'm stuck in a time warp of some sort. Or a make-believe land where everything is perfect all the time, like Stepford, if Stepford had tourists and a beach. I long for a good thunderstorm (which I've been told we've had once or twice, but they came and went so fast I missed them). Better yet, a blizzard. I mean, it's three days until Christmas and here I am, in my bare feet, walking along the ocean, cool sand squishing between my toes, gentle water lapping over my ankles if I let it. I miss snow and cold more than I expected to.

Of course, thinking of snow and cold leads me to thinking about Christmas. Thinking about Christmas has me missing my family and missing Kim, which sends me into a weird spiral of analysis, which causes a strange question to hit my subconscious.

Do I miss Kim?

I mean, do I *really* miss her?

I stop walking for a moment, my steps faltering as the question enters my consciousness, and for some reason I cannot pinpoint, I consider how I'd rather be thinking about missing my mom than missing my ex. It's a weird mental battle that goes on in my brain, but I somehow understand that the thing I don't want to focus on needs my focus. I continue walking as I make myself really think about it—*really* think about it. It's a weird awareness that's been creeping in over the past day or two, and I know I've been avoiding it. It is simply this: do I miss Kim or do I miss the *idea* of what Kim and I were, what we were going to have, what we were going to be? Is it possible I miss the whole having a big wedding, being the center of attention for a day, actually being married thing more than I truly miss my girlfriend? Ex-girlfriend, I mean. Let's be honest, I was kissing somebody else last night. How much can I possibly be missing Kim if I was so into sticking my tongue down another woman's throat? Kim's text was inconsiderate and hurtful, yes, but am I acting like somebody who was, for all intents and purposes, left at the altar?

I'm not sure.

I stop again, let the thought replay.

I'm not sure.

I cock my head as if listening to a far-off sound, and wonder what the hell I've been thinking all this time. Kim and I weren't together for very long. A year and a half. Seems long enough to know whether or not you want to marry somebody, doesn't it? I was sure. That I know. I was sure I wanted to get married. I wanted to wear white. I wanted my dad to walk me down the aisle. I wanted to recite my self-written vows in front of all my friends and family. But now that I'm really thinking about it, does Kim show up anywhere in that picture? Or is it just a faceless somebody as my partner?

It's not a happy thing to realize about yourself, I can tell you that right now. Understanding that maybe you didn't really have the right priorities in life is a nasty slap in the face. I know because it cracks me one right then and there on the beach in Florida on my freaking un-honeymoon, so much so that I actually stagger back a step.

"Oh, Christ," I mutter, and an older gentleman glances my way as he passes me in the sand. I try to give him a reassuring smile, but I'm sure I grimace instead. He probably wonders if I ate a bad clam.

Allison.

I need to talk to Allison about this. She'll understand. She'll help me to understand. Maybe she'll even tell me that I'm not a completely self-centered bridezilla...though that may be asking a lot. She's pretty honest, and if I ask her not to spare me, she won't.

I spin on my heel and begin walking back the way I came. I'm startled to see how far I've managed to walk. The resort is nothing more than a few glimmers of gold trim reflecting the setting sun. As a handsome couple of men approach me, I see one is wearing a watch (not terribly common any more), and I ask him for the time. When he tells me, I realize I promised Allison I'd be gone for half an hour, but it's already been forty-five minutes, and I still have another twenty minutes of walking to do. And yet again, I've left my phone in my room.

I pick up the pace.

Chapter Fifteen

IT'S FUNNY HOW, WHEN you're not paying attention to where you're wandering, you can seemingly get really far in a short period of time, but when you're hurrying to get somewhere, it can take infinitely longer than you think it should.

I'm practically jogging down the beach back to the hotel. And I hate to jog. But I don't want Allison to worry about me. Worse, I don't want her to think I blew her off after I promised I wouldn't. And I can't decide if I want to drag her off to a corner and pick her brain about all the crap I just analyzed about myself or just drink and dance the night away and not worry about it right now. It really is a toss-up.

The sun is a bright marble of reddish-orange, and it's just disappearing over the water, and it's stunning. If I wasn't in such a hurry to get back, I'd stop for an extra moment or two and just look at it. But the sense of urgency I suddenly feel is too much, and I plow forward as quickly as I can.

The resort is hopping, and I remember it's the weekend. Days tend to blend into one another for me when I'm on vacation, and I lose track. I wander hallways and large, open common areas until I reach one of those map thingies like they have in the mall to help you find just exactly where Bath & Body Works is so you can make sure to use your coupon replenishing your bubble bath before it expires tomorrow. Not that I've ever done that. I run my finger over the different colored blocks, trying to figure out where I am in conjunction with Night Moves because I think I've gotten myself turned around. I definitely came in a different set of doors than I left through, and that's throwing me off.

"This place is freaking enormous," a guy says as he sidles up next to me. I like his aftershave.

I chuckle. "I know, right? I've been here for three days, and I'm still lost."

"Are you having a good time?" he asks me. "We just got here. Still finding our footing." He holds out his hand and a man I assume to be his partner takes it. They're both clean cut, lean, and tan.

"I'm having a great time," I tell him, and I'm surprised to realize that I mean it. Soul-searching and over-indulging aside, I am truly glad I came. It's an interesting fact that brings a genuine smile to my face. I hope they don't think I'm rude as I keep running my finger along the map, studying it, hoping they'll get the hint that I'm in a hurry and don't really have time to chat.

They look excited as they thank me and continue on their way. I go back to following my finger as it slides along until I figure out where the hell I am. I see I'm diagonal across the main floor from where I want to be, so I head off in what I hope is the right direction.

I turn the corner, pretty sure I'm heading the right way, and I pass a bank of elevators. One of them dings as I approach and spills its contents out in front of me: a handful of about four women looking like they're ready for a night of drinking and dancing. They're laughing and they're loud, and it makes me smile. A blonde woman of average height is wearing a black camp shirt over her white T-shirt. She glances in my direction and her eyes widen slightly as if she recognizes me.

"Hey there," she says, and I actually look over my shoulder to see who behind me she's talking to. She is completely unfamiliar to me, but she is addressing me. "You look a thousand times better than the last time we saw you." She taps the woman next to her on the shoulder. "Doesn't she, Mia?"

Mia has short, dark hair and very dark eyes. She turns them on me and the same widening occurs. "Oh, yeah. Way better. How are you?"

I can't do much more than blink because I have no idea who they are. "I'm good?" I say, and it's almost a question because I'm confused. "I'm sorry, when was the last time you saw me?"

"Last night," the blonde tells me.

Oh, shit. I groan, wondering what exactly these women saw, and at the same time not wanting to know. Will this never stop? Is there an endless line of strangers who will continue to bump into me and tell me what embarrassing things I did last night?

To Mia, the blonde says, "Told you she wouldn't remember." Then back to me, "I gave you my bottle of water. In the elevator."

A memory tickles the back of my mind, but no flash of picture comes forth, which I find very frustrating. "Oh, my god. I'm so embarrassed. That's not…" My voice trails off because I'm torn between explaining my entire situation (is there a better reason to get plowed at a bar than it being your wedding day, except you didn't get married?) and turning to run away as fast as I possibly can. I can feel the heat rising up my neck and into my cheeks. "That's not how I usually…I don't get…I'm just not…ugh." I hang my head and slowly shake it from side to side.

The blonde laughs and grabs my upper arm with her warm hand, gives me a gentle squeeze. "Oh, honey. We've all been there, believe me. You have nothing to be ashamed about. You were actually kind of cute." I finally look up to meet her eyes and she winks. "And if that sexy caretaker there was taking you back to the room, I suspect you were all set. She was hot."

Mia agrees with an enthusiastic nod of her head. "She was *so* hot."

I allow a smile to pull up one corner of my mouth and silently wonder if Frankie has that effect on every woman she comes across.

"Is she yours, I assume?" the blonde asks me, adding another wink for good measure. "Those eyes. Such a deep blue."

"And kind of intense," Mia adds. "I think she was worried about you."

"Really?" My heart warms a bit, which is good because I'm hoping it'll take some of the heat out of my face, which is burning up as I listen to the effort Frankie had to put forth in order to get me back to my room...and then not even get any type of reward. I suck. Completely.

"Yeah, she kept trying to make you laugh." Mia glances at the blonde. "She even had *you* going a couple times."

The blonde chuckles. "She did. I have to admit it. I am not normally a fan of blonde jokes," she points to her head, "for obvious reasons, but she had some good ones."

I furrow my brow. "Wait. What?"

"Two blondes fall down a hole," Mia begins animatedly. "One of them says, 'It's dark in here, isn't it?' The other answers—."

"I don't know, I can't see," they say together, then bust into tandem laughter.

"No," I say, more to myself than to them. "That can't be right."

"Wait, wait...what was that other one? The roof one?"

Mia laughs harder. "How do you get a blonde up on the roof?"

Again, they both give the punch line together. "Tell her drinks are on the house!" They dissolve into more laughter.

"I'm sorry, can you tell me..." I wait for them to collect themselves before I continue. "Can you tell me what she looked like?"

Mia blinks at me. "You don't remember her? At all? Oh, honey, you *were* schnockered, weren't you? That's what my grandpa calls it. Schnockered."

"I love your grandpa," the blonde says.

"Please." I'm just shy of dropping to my knees and begging them to hurry. I feel like my world has just tilted sideways, and I'm working overtime to maintain my balance, knowing I could slide off at any moment. "Please. What did she look like?"

They look at each other as if confirming.

"About this tall," Mia says, holding her hand up to what would be about 5'6", and the blonde nods her agreement. "Dark hair. Blue eyes."

"Gorgeous blue eyes," the blond clarifies.

"Short hair?" I ask.

"Short-ish," the blonde says. "About to here." She slices her hand just above her shoulders.

I swallow. "Spiked in the front?" *Please say yes. Please say yes. Please say yes.*

"No, not at all. Nicely styled, but it looked soft, not stiff like those spikey cuts tend to."

"She had the cutest little dimple in her chin," Mia says.

"Cleft," the blonde corrects her.

"What?" Mia says.

"It's called a cleft when it's on your chin. Not a dimple."

"Whatever. A cleft. She had a cleft in her chin. That and her eyes, those are what I remember most clearly. She was sexy."

"Oh, my god," I say, then cover my mouth with my hand.

"Don't worry, sweetie. She was taking good care of you and seemed very sweet. She held you up on your feet…and that was easier said than done. Kept her arms around you the whole time, and like I said, she seemed very concerned about you. What in the world did you have to drink anyway?"

At that point, flashes of memory do start to hit, but they're still not totally clear. I can see the inside of the elevator now, the bottle of water in my hand, I can hear laughter. It's all so soft-edged and out of focus, but in my mind, my head is bowed. All I can see is the floor…I squeeze my eyes shut, open them again, look up into a tender smile, loving blue eyes.

Allison's eyes.

"Oh, my god," I say again, and I literally spin in a circle as I look for the right direction. I have to find Allison. "Why didn't she tell me?" I say.

"Tell you what, honey?" The blonde's voice has an edge of concern in it.

"Hey, are you okay?" Mia asks, reaching for my shoulder.

I feel like I'm going to throw up. Allison was in the elevator with me last night, which means Frankie wasn't. So it only makes sense that Allison was the one holding my hair while I threw up like a college coed. I look directly at the two women and say again, "Why didn't she tell me?"

They shake their heads in tandem, I'm sure at a total loss as to what's going on with me. I have the irrational urge to laugh out loud at the picture they've gotten of me over the past twenty-four hours. I will definitely be a topic of conversation when they get home and tell their friends about their vacation.

There was this woman…what a mess she was! First, we saw her in the elevator and she was three sheets to the wind. Couldn't even stand up on her own. But she had this hot brunette taking care of her.

Not that she noticed because she was drunker than a groom at his bachelor party. Then we ran into her the next day, and not only did she not remember us, she didn't even remember the woman who got her to her room! A total blackout drunk. Man, she had some problems. I hope she gets some therapy...

I could benefit from some therapy right about now because I am so utterly confused. I need to find Frankie. I need to find Allison. I need to find a rock to crawl under.

Unable to stand there any longer, I touch the blonde's arm and say, "Thank you so much for the water. It was really nice of you. Bye." And then I spin on my heel and walk in what I hope is the right direction. What I really want to do is sprint, but the combination of how that would look and the fact that the floor is polished marble and I'm wearing smooth-soled flip-flops keep me walking at a reasonable speed.

"Did this place grow overnight?" I mutter, annoyed that I feel like I've been walking for five years. "What the hell?" The rational part of my brain knows that it's fine, I'm going in the right direction, the club will show up soon. The irrational part (which seems ridiculously loud and powerful right now) wants to shriek, to just stand here and scream until somebody comes up to me to ask what I want, and I can just tell them and have them get it for me. I feel like a toddler, completely frustrated and confused and angry.

"Okay, Mackenzie," I whisper to myself. "Chill. Find the club. Get to the bottom of things. It's fine. You're fine. Just chill. The fuck. Out." I take a deep breath, slow my pace, and begin to pick up the throbbing bass beat that surely must be coming from Night Moves. I follow the sound for another three minutes and there it is. "Thank god."

I step through the doorway and it's as if I'm plunged into a basement. It's so dark. They've got the fluorescent black lights on, so all I can make out clearly is anything white. Lots of shoes. Thousands of teeth. The occasional shirt here and there. Some nail polish. I wander through the crowd—which seems three times the size it was the first night we were here—and scan the people, the faces, trying to find one I recognize. I'm just starting to get anxious when I hear my name. I squint in the direction I think it came from, and I see an arm with some brightly glowing bracelets waving at me. As I approach, I see it's Jules. Thank god.

"Hey," she says. Or rather, she shouts, as the music is so loud I can barely hear myself think. Jules is bopping up and down, dancing without being on the dance floor. "Come on!" She grabs my hand and begins tugging me in that direction, but I put on the brakes.

"Where's Allison?" I ask at the top of my lungs.

Jules squints at me.

"Allison!" I try again. "Where is Allison?"

"She went looking for you." Jules wags a playfully scolding finger at me. "You were gone for a long time, young lady."

"I know. I walked farther down the beach than I thought." Jules is still bopping, her gaze drifting back to the dance floor, and I'm worried she's not listening to me. I tug at her shirt to get her attention. "Do you know where she went?"

Jules shakes her head. "Sure you don't want to dance?" She's backing away from me toward the dance floor, cricking her finger at me in a come-hither gesture. If I wasn't freaking out, I'd laugh and join her.

"Later," I mouth because I know she's too far away to hear me now. Then I turn away and head in the direction of the door. The crowd has closed the path I used to get where I am, and I feel like a salmon swimming upstream trying to get through. As I'm pushing past the bar, I glance to my left, and a familiar face catches my eye. I narrow my gaze, then change directions.

Frankie looks good. In fact, she looks great, even in just black light. As if hearing my thoughts, the regular lighting comes back on...not much brighter, but it's a lot easier to see detail. She's wearing tight black jeans with boots. Her white button-down shirt looks like the sleeves have been cut off, which serve to show the well-developed muscles of her arms. It occurs to me that she must work out in addition to giving massages. Her hair is perfect, not a strand out of place, neat on the sides, spiked up a bit in the front, and glistening from whatever hair product she's put in it. She's leaning one elbow on the bar, talking to a pretty little blonde thing whose expression shows just exactly how enamored she is with Frankie. I immediately wonder if I looked that naïve when I was in her place. Probably. I sigh, embarrassed for the blonde and for me.

Then Frankie reaches into a pocket and pulls out a little plant clipping, and it's like the groan and eye roll I produce are all done without my permission. I stomp toward them, grab Frankie's arm, and pull her away, as she burps a girly little, "Hey!" of protest.

"Jesus Christ," I say in disgust once we hit a somewhat private corner. "The mistletoe again?"

"What's your problem?" Her blue eyes spark, and god damn her, she's still sexy.

I point to the mistletoe. "*That* is my problem. Nice originality."

Frankie puffs out her chest like she's trying to stand taller. "Hey, worked on you, didn't it?"

I bite back a snotty reply because she's right. I totally thought that was charming last night. How could I not see it for what it was? "Is that one fresh out of a relationship, too?" I ask, gesturing at the pretty little blonde with my chin.

"Why? You jealous?"

I snort. "No. Not anymore. I was just wondering if that's your target audience...heartbroken with shattered self-esteem."

Frankie presses her lips together in a tight line and stares at me for a moment. "Look. A lot of women like you come here. They're sad. They've had their hearts stomped on. They think they're undesirable, that nobody wants them. I show them that it's not true. I don't see anything wrong with that. I never promise them anything more than what I can give: a hot night of passion."

For a split second, she has me. Her words are sincere—I firmly believe that *she* believes them—but it only takes a blink for me to understand that the main person getting what they want here is Frankie.

I bark a laugh. "You're a pig."

She takes a half-step backwards. "Fuck you."

"No, sadly, I've come to my senses," I say.

"Too bad for you. You would have loved it."

I grab her wrist before she can turn and leave, and I nod and try to grin. Because I think she's right. No, I know she's right. Most likely, I would have had a great time rolling in the hay with Frankie. I also probably would have wanted to crawl in a hole the next morning, but I keep that tidbit tamped down.

"You know what? I probably would have," I say to her, softer now. She stares me down for a moment before her face relaxes. "Listen, can you tell me about last night?"

Her dark brows meet above her nose. "What do you mean?"

I sigh, and my eyes slide away from hers as I swallow down my humiliation. "I was...pretty drunk."

Frankie scoffs, but wisely says nothing.

"I know, I know. I'm not proud of it. The rum runners snuck up on me, what can I say?"

"Yeah, they do that."

"All this time, I thought you took me back to my room…" I'm not sure how to phrase the rest of what I want to say. Hell, I don't even know what else I want to say, but I need all the pieces to the puzzle before I can put it together, and right now, I'm sure I'm missing, like, a lot of them.

Frankie looks off into the distance as she talks. "I would have. Believe me. I would have. You were adorable and sexy, even as plowed as you were. But I couldn't get past your guard dog." She says the last two words with disdain.

"My what?"

"Your guard dog. That's how I think of her because I thought she was going to take my arm off with her teeth." Frankie shakes her head in disgust, but I can see the mortification behind her eyes, and I almost laugh. She got cock-blocked, and she did not like it.

"What did she say? This guard dog of mine?"

"I don't even remember," Frankie says, but her expression tells me she's lying, that she remembers exactly what was said, probably word for word. "She just pushed me away from you, told me to leave you alone, that she'd take care of things from here." She gives a shrug to emphasize how much it was no big deal. "It was fine. You were hammered anyway. Nothing was going to happen."

I roll my lips in and bite on them for a second while I try to skip past what Frankie just said, try to absorb that I was really nothing but a prospective lay for her. Which I knew, if I'm being honest with myself. I certainly didn't think we'd fall into some deep, intense relationship. I go home after the holidays. Frankie stays here. I'm not naïve. But actually having the facts presented to me, to *clearly* understand that I wasn't any more than a wet vagina and a pair of boobs to somebody, is hard to swallow.

"You know," I say to Frankie once I feel like I can speak without either screaming in anger or crying in humiliation. "All this time, I thought you were the one who helped me out of here and kept me upright in the elevator, who took me back to my room, who held my head when I got sick, who got me out of my clothes and tucked me into bed. I was disappointed when you weren't with me this morning and I couldn't thank you. That's why I came looking for you. To thank you."

Frankie looks decidedly uncomfortable, but I give her credit for standing here and listening to me rather than telling me to fuck off and heading back to her latest challenge, who is still waiting for her, watching us closely.

"And now I find out that you don't even deserve my thanks. I spent an entire day of my vacation trying to hunt down somebody to show them my appreciation, and they don't even deserve it." Something occurs to me then. "Who was that woman you were with when I saw you earlier?"

Frankie clears her throat, doesn't meet my eyes. "That's my girlfriend."

I can feel my eyebrows raise up toward my hairline. "Excuse me?"

"My girlfriend. Of eight years."

I blink at her for what feels like ages. "Wow. I can honestly say I did not see that one coming." A bevy of information hits me then as pieces fall into place, and I actually laugh out loud. "Oh my god, she must have thought I was one of your little conquests, all broken-hearted and trying to find you to profess my undying love."

Frankie gives me a look. "It happens."

I shake my head. "That poor woman."

"We have an understanding."

"God, I hope so. And I hope she gets off as often as you do."

Frankie has no response other than to poke at the inside of her cheek with her tongue. I suspect she's trying to stay nice to me. After all, what would happen if I ran to her superiors and lodged a complaint?

I tilt my head to the side and study her for a moment. "You know what?"

"What?"

"I think I owe you my thanks after all."

She squints at me, as if she's unsure she wants to hear this.

I nod. "Yeah. I do. My time with you—and my time trying to find you—have helped me to understand my own worth." I take a second to breathe, because I'm actually beginning to understand that this is the truth. "Being left sucks, let me just tell you. It sucks in a big way, especially when you're left for somebody else. You feel worthless. Unwanted. Unattractive. It sounds a little ridiculous, I know. Kind of pathetic. Somebody like you wouldn't understand because I bet you've never been left. You've always done the leaving. That's smart. Keep control. Don't let anybody decide how your life is going to go." I swallow, look at her. She's not looking back at me, but again, I give her credit for standing here and letting me dress her down. "But somebody like me...we're in a different place. We're low, way down low, wondering if anybody will ever even *see* us again. Because if that last person didn't want us, why should anybody else? So we flounder and we struggle and we do what we can just to stay afloat, just to get through the day.

And then somebody like you comes along. Somebody charming and attractive and sexy and attentive. And, like you said, you make us feel like maybe—just maybe—we're not as ugly and undesirable as we thought. You give us hope. You make us feel alive again."

Frankie is looking at me now, and her face says she's feeling some pride, that this assessment of her is good. I hold up a finger.

"Oh, no. Don't get all peacocky. Because you're just as bad as the person who left us in the first place. No, you're worse. You make us feel all those things again, but you're just using us. For sex. And we don't know it until the next morning when you either make some excuse and run away as fast as you can, then avoid us for the rest of our vacation, or you sneak out in the middle of the night, after you've gotten what you wanted.

"I escaped, though. You see? Not by my own brilliance, unfortunately, but it doesn't matter. I still escaped you. You didn't send me crashing back down into my hole of despair again like you do to so many women. Because I'm better than that. I'm better than you. I owe you, Frankie. You've helped me to understand that I'm better than the person Kim made me feel like I was." I step toward her, kiss her gently on the cheek, then step back. "Thank you." I hold her gaze for a beat. "And now I'm going to go find my guard dog so I can thank her, too."

I can't think of a more satisfying moment in all of my life than right then, Frankie watching me walk away from her, her expression a mix of disbelief, confusion, anger, and embarrassment. As I pass the pretty little blonde, I pat her on the shoulder, tell her, "You can do better," and leave Night Moves behind.

I need to have a few words with Allison.

Chapter Sixteen

I HAVEN'T HAD ANY trouble getting around The Rainbow's Edge since I got here, despite the gargantuan size of the place. I've taken the right elevators, turned the right corners, found the right doorways any time I was looking for someplace, and the crowds have been minimal.

Except for today.

"Jesus Christ," I mutter as I try to push my way through the lobby. It's as if half the guests have decided to hang out here and converse while standing right in my path. Every one of them chattering away, nobody noticing my approach, nobody giving me the time of day until I say—loudly and probably a little ruder than necessary—"Excuse me, please." Many a dirty look is tossed my way, but I don't care. Again, feeling like the proverbial salmon swimming upstream, I push and push and push until it's as though I'm propelled out of the crowd and skid to a stop in front of the elevators. I'm surprised there isn't a *pop* to go along with the feeling of being shot out of a bottle.

I push the up button and wait. And wait. And wait. Finally looking up, I see that the elevator must have started on the nineteenth floor. The other three cars are moving in the opposite direction.

"Seriously?" I say aloud, beginning to believe that the Universe is totally fucking with me. I bounce up and down on the balls of my feet while trying to sort out all the crap that is suddenly clogging up my brain.

Allison took care of me last night. Allison.

Why didn't she tell me?

I squeeze my eyes shut and focus on the memories, still only coming in bits and pieces.

Stumbling through the door of the room, literally, while strong hands keep me upright. I can feel them on my upper arm and around my waist, but my savior is behind me.

"Here. Drink this." A bottle of water is put to my lips, and I obey. And the voice is alarmingly familiar (now).

On my knees in the bathroom, hugging the bowl, crying.

"Oh, god." I shake my head, embarrassed all over again. The elevator door dings, finally, and I hop on. Miraculously, nobody boards with me. I punch the button for my floor at the same time as a suddenly crystal clear memory from last night punches me in the stomach.

I'm on the floor in the bathroom. No idea how long I've been here, but I'm hugging the bowl with my arm and my view is not pretty. I've obviously unloaded once already. The smell is revolting. My nose is running. I'm on the verge of tears.

"It's okay, sweetie," Allison is saying. "It's okay. Get it all out."

She's holding my hair back; I can feel her hand at the back of my head, her grip gentle. With her other hand, she's rubbing my back in soothing circles.

I retch. Enough liquid comes out of my stomach to float a small canoe. I cough, but the coughing soon morphs into sobs, and I'm crying in earnest now.

"What's wrong with me, Allie? I don't understand." I sound so sad, even now in my own head. "I don't understand," I say again, shaking my head back and forth.

Allison's voice is suddenly closer, and I sense that she's kneeled down next to me. "Nothing," she says, and I can't remember ever hearing her sound so adamant. "Nothing is wrong with you." She kisses my temple tenderly, continues to rub my back.

"Then why?" I wail. It's melodramatic in my memory and I suspect it was in reality, too, but I can sense my own pain, the recollection of it poking at my heart. *"Why do women keep hurting me? What did I do? Am I bad? Am I a bad person?"*

"You're not a bad person." I recognize the slightly patronizing tone of Allison's voice. After all, I was very, very drunk. I probably asked the same question over and over. *"You're an amazing person."*

I turn away from the bowl, lay my arm across it so I can rest my head on my arm as I try to focus on my friend. Even in my memory, her face is blurry. (I am never drinking rum again. Ever.) *"I am?"*

Allison gently pushes some hair off my face, strokes a thumb across my eyebrow. I close my eyes and soak in the joy of being touched lovingly by somebody else. "You are more than amazing, Mackenzie. You're the most wonderful person I've ever met."

"I am?"

"You are." Allison shifts so she's sitting on the floor instead of squatting, and she continues to play with my hair as she speaks. *"You're smart and funny and kind. You have a big heart and a terrific sense of humor. There are so many things to love about you."*

"Like what?"

"I love that you cry over Hallmark commercials. I love that you can watch "The Golden Girls" on an endless loop and laugh every time. I love that you wouldn't be able to toss a shirt into the hamper inside out even with a gun to your head. I love that you have no idea how beautiful you are. I love that you can't hold your liquor."

I give a little bark of a laugh at that. "I am so drunk."

"I know. It's okay."

"Kim left me."

"Kim's an idiot."

"She doesn't love me."

"Doesn't matter. I love you."

"You do?"

"I always have."

My eyes pop open, causing me to lose the rest of the memory. My heart is hammering in my chest. Did I remember that right? God, I was so intoxicated. I can't trust my memory, though in my experience, usually what comes back in bits and pieces is fairly accurate.

"Um…are you coming out? No pun intended."

I snap my gaze up to the two women standing outside the open elevator door, one of them with her hand preventing the doors from sliding closed. I didn't even hear the ding announcing my floor.

"Oh. Yeah. Sorry." I step out into the hallway. "Thanks."

The woman nods and the two of them get in the car. I blink at them as the doors slide closed. I have no idea how much time passes as I stand there and try my best to wring more memories from my head. It's not happening, though, and I accept the fact that there's only one way to get to the bottom of all of this.

Spinning on my heel, I head down the hall towards my room.

I hope she's here. I don't want to spend the entire night searching for people. First Frankie. Now Allison. I'm exhausted. My eyes hurt. My head is filled to capacity. I can't take any more.

I slide my key card in, get the green light, and enter.

Allison is perched at the foot of the enormous bed, her gaze focused on something out the window. Or maybe not focused at all, I can't tell. Her bag is open next to her, almost filled with all of her stuff. A sick feeling hits my stomach immediately, but I decide I'll address the bag later.

"Hi," I say and curl my leg up under me as I sit on the side of the bed.

"Hi," she says, not looking at me.

"Hey, why does the new Polish navy have glass-bottomed boats?"

Allison lifts one shoulder.

"So they can see the old Polish navy."

The little puff of breath she releases serves as a chuckle.

"Sorry I was gone so long," I say. "I got carried away on my beach walk. For some reason, it seemed to take a lot longer to get back."

"No problem."

We sit in silence for a long moment.

"Allison…was it you?" I ask quietly, tracing the pattern of the comforter with my finger. "Last night?"

Her swallow is audible. "Was what me?"

"Was it you who took care of me?"

She nods, very slowly.

"All of it? You got me back here? Made sure I had water? Held my hair?"

"Listened to you puke. Listened to you cry. Made you take some aspirin."

"Took my clothes off?"

Allison turns to me then, a pink flush decorating her cheekbones. "You'd gotten puke on your shirt, so I got you out of it, and then *you* kept undressing. I got you some pajamas, but you wouldn't put them on." She looks almost horrified, as if I'd implied her intentions were untoward.

I smile in the hopes of easing her discomfort. "I don't wear pajamas at home. I'm sure I had no idea where I was."

"Oh. Well. You were all about wanting to be naked."

I think about that. Allison and I are the best of friends, but as I said before, when you're both lesbians, there are a few things you don't do in the presence of the other. One is undress. I've never seen her naked, and she's never seen me. Well, she *had* never seen me. I guess I took care of that. Twice on this trip, in fact.

"You let me think it was Frankie all this time." I'm not accusing her. It's a statement of fact. A baffling one, but a statement just the same.

Allison gives the one-shoulder shrug again. "Seems like that's what you wanted to believe. Who am I to take that from you?"

I squint at her, not sure what to make of that. Then something occurs to me. "You didn't set up the chastity pillows. That's why I thought she'd been here. Maybe spooning with me. Cuddling so I wouldn't feel alone. I get a little lonely and clingy when I've been drinking, and—"

Allison's head whips around to snag me in her gaze as she interrupts my rambling. "*I* spooned you. *I* did," she snaps. "There were no pillows because you asked me to cuddle with you. You said you were lonely and that your heart was broken, and would I please, please just hold you. *You asked me to.*"

My mouth opens and closes several times before any sound comes out. Even then, it's not much. "Oh."

"Yeah. You slept practically wrapped around me like some kind of human vine of ivy or something. A *naked* vine of ivy."

She's turned away from me again, and I tug on my bottom lip, trying with little success to fill in the rest of the night. (I am never drinking rum again. Ever.) I keep coming back to the same sticking point.

"You let me think it was Frankie," I say for the second time.

Allison clears her throat, and gives me a slightly varied version of the same answer she already gave. "It was what you wanted. You assumed she'd been the one to…help, and you seemed so pleased by the idea that it was her. What was I supposed to do, Kenz? Tell you the truth? Tell you that the second Frankie's chances of getting into your pants dwindled, she was no longer interested in you? That you were nothing but a piece of ass to her right from the beginning? Why would I do that to you?"

It feels like she's trying to hurt me. I think she is. I already know all of this about Frankie, but to hear it come out of Allison's mouth that way stings. A split second of satisfaction zips across her face before it's replaced by regret. Allison is not mean-spirited. She's not vindictive. She hurt me. She knows it. She feels bad.

"Why didn't you just tell me it was you?" I ask, my voice small.

She startles me when she literally jumps off the bed. "*Because it's always me!*" she yells. Her blue eyes are crackling with emotion: fire, pain, despair. I feel suddenly awful, though I haven't yet figured out why. "It's always me," she says again, much softer this time. "And I'm done."

She snaps her bag closed and zips it up. She puts it on the floor and telescopes the handle. I'm speechless, as I'm not a hundred percent sure what just happened. It's always her? What does she mean? I hold out a hand, which she deftly avoids.

"Allie, wait."

"I can't, Kenzie. It's too hard. I just…I can't."

Like an idiot, I watch her walk out of the room, the door clicking shut behind her.

It's late.

It's late and I'm frigging exhausted, and I'm confused. I know, as I flop back onto the bed, that I need to talk more with Allison. She sort of lost me right after the "you asked me to cuddle with you" part of the explanations from last night…mostly because the picture that suddenly jumped into my head of the cuddling was really distracting and not at all unpleasant.

I've thought about Allison that way. Of course I have. Anybody who's seen her has. She's gorgeous. She's gorgeous and she's smart and she's sexy and she's self-assured. Lots of "s" descriptors there, but you get my point. Allison is very attractive. She's the total package.

But for the past four years, we've been friends. And three of those years, she was with Marianne. So what difference would it have made if I thought of her that way? Nothing would have happened. She was attached when I was single. When I became attached, she ended up single. Obviously, the Universe has something different in mind for us. Right? Otherwise, the planets would have aligned or whatever the hell is supposed to happen when Fate works its magic. And then it would have worked out. Right? But it didn't.

I should get up. I blow out a weary breath and try saying it out loud.

"Get up."

No magical hands appear in the air to pull me to a sitting position, so I lay there as the night grows deeper. I'm just so damn tired.

I'm sure Allison just took her stuff to Jules' room and will stay there for the night. I'm worried about her. I've never seen her so upset, not even after she and Marianne broke up. Sure, she was sad, but she was nowhere near the emotional devastation that I experienced a couple weeks ago.

God, was it only a couple weeks ago? I feel like I've been on my own, without Kim, for years. Isn't that weird? I close my eyes and try to let all the stress drain out of me. It's a move a friend at work taught me. She teaches yoga on the side, and at the end of each class, she has her students lay on their backs, close their eyes, and start at their heads, working their way down through each body part, mentally willing the stress to just drain out of their bodies and into the floor. I've become rather good at it.

I start with my skull, my scalp, picturing all the tension just rolling off my head.

I love you.

You do?

I always have.

My neck and shoulders. I carry much of my stress here, so I spend extra time talking myself into relaxation, turning them into mental jelly.

You were all about being naked.

My torso. As I've said, my stomach is the other place of stress. Any tension that's not in my neck and shoulders centers in my stomach. I focus on stillness. Peace.

You said you were lonely and that your heart was broken, and would I please, please just hold you. You asked me to.

My arms and hands. It's really the easiest part of the body to do. I wiggle my fingers, stretch the muscles in my arms.

Because it's always me!

Hips and legs. Almost as easy as the arms, but my glutes can sometimes tighten up without my even realizing it. I take a deep breath and concentrate.

It's always me. And I'm done.

My feet. The bottom. The end. The last in the list. I center my focus, but open my eyes. The curtains are wide open, and I can see the ocean. I take a deep breath, close my eyes again, concentrate on my feet, and try to forget the echoes of Allison's voice in my head.

Sleep claims me.

163

Chapter Seventeen

THINGS ARE SUPPOSED TO be better in the morning, aren't they? Fresher? Clearer?

What a bunch of horse shit.

I wake up with yet another pounding headache, but without the benefit or mystery of a possibly awesome time had the night before. I'm lying across the foot of the bed, and at some point during the night, I must have gotten chilly and grabbed the comforter to cover myself because I'm rolled up like a burrito, and it takes me a good minute or two to free myself from the swaddling.

I sit up, and that's as far as I get for a bit, letting my feet dangle, noticing for the first time how ridiculously large this bed is. For a minute, I wonder why wouldn't you put a smaller bed in the Honeymoon Suite? Isn't the point of your honeymoon to have sex and be as close as possible? This bed is so enormous, I could lay on one side, stretch my arm fully out to the side, and not touch the person sleeping on the other side. What does a bed the size of an airport runway have to do with a honeymoon?

I scrub my hand over my face and glance at the clock, stunned to see that it's after ten. I never sleep this late, even when I'm home in my own bed and have the day off, yet I've done it twice since I've been here. My mother always says your body won't sleep longer than it needs to, and if you sleep late, your body needed it. This is a good example.

Outside the window, the sun is brightly shining. I get up, wander to the balcony, and go out onto it. The ocean rushes in the distance, people wander the beach, traffic seems thin. I remember then that it's Sunday, and only three days before Christmas (I'm still counting today). A weird melancholy comes over me, and for a moment, I want nothing more than to be home, sitting in my mother's kitchen, helping her make Christmas cookies and talking about what food she's decided on this year for Christmas Day.

My eyes fill.

In the bathroom, I make the mistake of looking in the mirror. Seriously, when will I learn? I am not an unattractive woman. I know this. But I think Florida hates me because I've looked nothing but tired, haggard, and hung over since I got here. My blonde hair is matted on one side and ratty on the other. My normally clear blue eyes are cloudy and accentuated by those lovely dark circles underneath. My cheeks seem sunken and the overall tone of my skin seems sallow. What the hell?

I sigh, strip, and step into the shower, the water as hot as I can possibly stand it.

Have you ever tried to actively *not* think about something? Like, you get in the shower or your car or whatever, and you say to yourself (sometimes out loud), "I am not going to think about such-and-such right now." Ever do that? Does it work for you? Yeah, me neither. Because I get in the shower and tell myself (out loud), "I am not going to think about this thing with Allison right now. My brain is too fried, and I have no idea what I'm going to do. I need a moment's peace." And of course, where does my brain go? Right to Allison.

I recall our entire conversation last night. All of it. I think about the facts of Friday night. Not my airbrushed version of what happened, the facts of what really happened. Just the facts. I list them out:

I got blasted.

Frankie thought I'd make for a good lay.

Allison stepped in and scared Frankie off.

Allison helped me to the elevator (and was worried about me according to the water bottle-bearing duo we met there, so told me jokes to cheer me up).

I puked my guts out while Allison held my hair and sat with me on the bathroom floor.

I fell into Self-Pity Mode (a stellar reason to never get blasted again).

Allison told me she's always loved me. (I file that away for further examination.)

I stripped out of my clothes and paraded around naked. In front of Allison. (I bump my head against the shower tiles to reprimand myself.)

Allison put me to bed. And when I asked her to stay with me, she did.

I let my mind linger there…me in bed, no clothes on. Allison spooned up behind me, holding me tightly, never making any kind of move because she knows I'm in no state to handle such a thing.

And then another flash hits me. It's the seemingly insignificant memory of yesterday morning. Me waking up, trying to piece together the events of the previous night, Allison coming into the room with coffee for both of us, smiling, her eyes gentle and loving.

Then I asked her when Frankie left.

I've got to give her credit. She barely flinched. I remember seeing something in her face, but she hid it so well, and I was being such a thick-headed moron that I let it zip by. She never said anything. Why didn't she say something right then?

Well, that's an easy one.

She assumed I'd remember the night before.

I'd effectively crushed her because I hadn't.

And she gave me all day to figure it out.

Which, I didn't.

God, she must hate me. No wonder she wanted to get away from me.

With a heavy breath, I turn off the water, sure I've scalded off the top layer of my skin, and dry myself with the surprisingly thick towel. I wrap it around me, run a comb through my hair, add gel, and then pad back into the room to sit on the bed and contemplate some more.

I hate being so stuck inside my head. Kim used to say I *ruminated* on things too much. Ruminate? Really? What am I, eighty-five? I just like to think things through. There's nothing wrong with that. But often, I find I think too much. I spend too much time thinking and too little time doing. It's a habit I inherited from my father, so the best way to jumpstart things into motion is the get a good kick in the pants from my mother. She's been dealing with this behavior of my dad's for the better part of forty years.

I pick up my phone and scan for a text from Allison before I realize I'm doing it. Nothing, and it's more depressing than I expected. I swallow down a lump and call my mom.

"Hello there, sweetheart," she says by way of greeting. She's excessively cheerful, and I know it's because she wants me there. It'll get worse over the next three days, but as before, she's making a valiant attempt *not* to guilt-trip me. I know how hard that is for her, and I have to swallow down the lump again because her efforts touch me. "How's the weather there? Do I want to know? Am I going to hate you? We got six inches of snow last night."

I laugh. I can't help myself. In a crisis, there's nobody I want in my corner more than my mother. When you look up family loyalty in the dictionary, there's a picture of her there, I'm sure of it.

"I haven't been outside yet, but according to my balcony, it's warm, breezy, and sunny."

"I hate you."

"I know. Next time, you'll have to come with me."

"I'd like that."

"What are you up to? Which cookies do you still have to do?" I make small talk because I need to ease into the subject at hand. Mom knows I didn't call to check on her cookie making, but she plays along.

"I just have press cookies left. I'm doing those this afternoon, I think. Your father has a meeting."

I laugh because she just gave me two codes. Doing the press cookies last means my father has been on a cookie-eating rampage, and she had to wait in order to ensure there are any cookies to serve Christmas Day visitors. My dad has been retired for two years, so saying he has "a meeting" means he's meeting his golf buddies at a local bar for lunch.

"Use that big Tupperware container and hide the cookies in the closet where the vacuum cleaner is until Wednesday," I suggest. "He'll never look there."

She laughs, and the sound warms my heart. "You know, that's not a bad idea, honey."

There's a bit of a silent moment and then she asks, "How're you doing? You doing okay?"

I take a deep breath, and begin. "Well...I'm not sure." And then the whole story spills out. I tell her everything. It's one of the best and worst things about my relationship with my mom. I can tell her anything. She doesn't judge. She doesn't tell me how I should have done things differently (unless I ask). What she does is use things later. She can call up an inconsequential event from years ago and use it to make her point with frightening accuracy. I only hate it because it's not something I've ever been able to master.

I don't leave anything out. I tell her about Frankie and the massage and the mistletoe. I tell her about getting hammered by rum runners and how I was absolutely willing to end up on my back with Frankie, no matter how much alcohol I'd had. I tell her about waking up, Allison and the coffee, my frantic search for Frankie all day yesterday, about finding her, about the girlfriend. When I stop to take a breath, Mom interjects for the first time.

"It was Allison, wasn't it?" she asks.

I blink several times before I answer. "How could you possibly know that?" I'm baffled. Is my mother psychic and she just never told me? Is that how she always seems to know what I'm thinking?

"I pay attention, honey. Something you ought to try once in a while." There's a gentle lilt in her voice that takes away any sting, even though I squint and wonder if she just insulted me.

"What? What does that mean?"

"Mackenzie, you are a smart girl. You're very smart. I've always been so proud of you, your grades in school and in college, the way you interviewed and nailed the job you wanted. My daughter is incredibly intelligent."

"But...?" I know it's there. I can feel it coming.

"But sometimes, you are the dumbest smart girl I know."

"What? Mom! Jesus."

"Calm down. Calm down. All I'm saying is, you don't see things. You don't always pay attention to what's going on around you."

I'm shaking my head even though she can't see me. "I don't understand."

"I know you don't, honey. How long have you known Allison?"

"Four years, give or take a few weeks."

"And when did you two become best friends? How long has she been your person?"

"My what?"

"Your person." She sounds annoyed with me. "I thought you watched *Grey's Anatomy*. Your person. The one you turn to. The one who knows you best. Your person. How long has Allison been your person?"

"Oh. I don't know. Three years, maybe? Two or three?"

"And when did she break up with her last girlfriend?"

I answer slowly. "A little over a year ago."

"Mm hm. And has she been dating? At all?"

I stop to really think about the question. At home, I don't recall her seeing anybody since she moved out of her house with Marianne and into her own place. I flash quickly on Jules, on the Athletic Cutie from the pool, but in both cases, it seems like Allison has received attention, but hasn't pursued any. "No. Not really."

"Why do you think that is?" Mom is starting to sound impatient now.

"I don't know," I say, but I'm lying.

"Mackenzie. Honey. Have you never seen the way she looks at you?"

And there it is. I'm not sure if I was waiting for confirmation from an outside party or what, but I suddenly feel like all the pieces, they don't fall into place, they crash. Like bricks. No, like cinder blocks. Loud, heavy cinder blocks. "Oh."

"Yeah, oh," Mom says. "You know what else I've noticed?"

Do I even want to know? "What else have you noticed?"

"The way you look at her."

"What?" Now that surprises me.

"Can I tell you something without you getting mad at me?"

I swallow. Hard. "I don't know. Can you?"

"Well, I'm going to. Here it is: I was glad when Kim left you."

"*Mom!*"

"No, no, let me finish. Not because she broke your heart. I *hated* that she hurt you. I *hated* that she left you with such a mess." I could see my mom's face as she spoke, her eyebrows in a V above her nose, her teeth clenched together in anger. "And her timing couldn't have been worse. But." She stopped there, took an audible breath. "But I was happy that you didn't marry her. She wasn't right for you. Not when you were looking at another woman the way you look at Allison."

My eyes tear. I can't stop them. Good god, I've become a waterworks over the last couple of weeks. But it's as if hearing my mother say these things has validated all my insecurities, all my confusion, all my wondering why I don't miss Kim more. "Really? I didn't know you felt that way."

"Sweetie, it's not my place to tell you those things. You have to make your own way in the world, build your own life, make your own mistakes. But I was worried about you."

"Everything is such a mess, Mom." I can't help it; a sob burps out of me.

"Oh, honey. Shh. It's okay."

I cover my eyes with my hand and just let myself cry while my mom coos and murmurs soft words to me. She waits for my sobs to subside into little hiccups before she speaks again. "Where is Allison now?"

"I don't know. She took her bag and left last night. I think she went to Jules' room. They'd let her stay there, I'm sure."

"You need to find her, honey. Find her and talk about all of this. She deserves it, and so do you. I think you'll be surprised."

I drop my butt onto the bed, nodding even though she can't see me. I manage to mutter out a "'Kay," and it doesn't escape me that I sound like I'm twelve. "I will."

"You call me if you want to talk some more, okay?"

"I will."

"Promise me."

"I promise."

"I love you, baby. Now go figure all of this out. Okay?"

I nod again. "I love you, too, Mom. Thanks."

We hang up, and I sit and cry openly for a good while. In the back of my mind, I am sure my mother is home doing exactly the same thing. Me because my confusion is dissipating and I'm not sure if I'm too late to fix things. My mom because she's fifteen hundred miles away and can't help her daughter.

Merry Fucking Christmas.

Chapter Eighteen

IT'S FUNNY HOW YOUR perspective on a person or thing can change in the blink of an eye, isn't it? Maybe perspective is the wrong word. Outlook? Predictions? I'm not sure. All I know is that suddenly, I'm thinking about Allison differently. Well, maybe not thinking about her differently, but I'm revisiting in my head all the things we've done and said over the years, all the times I've noticed her for one reason or another, all the innocent flirting we've done as "friends." And I have questions. I have questions for her. I have questions for myself.

I've been good. As I said earlier, Allison is extremely attractive. I'm not blind. I've noticed. Many, many times I've noticed. But A, one of us was always with somebody, and B, I had no way of knowing if she thought of me like that. Mom thinks so. Mom says she sees the way Allison looks at me. Have I ever seen it?

A memory suddenly hits me. It was last Christmas at my place. Kim and I were having a get-together of a bunch of friends. Allison was fresh out of her relationship with Marianne, and had brought a friend she knew from college, just as company, not as a date. She seemed to be fine, though, given the fact that she'd just been through a break-up...content, smiling, drinking, but not to excess. I was in the kitchen opening a new bottle of wine, and I was blissful. I was in my gorgeous townhouse, I was surrounded by friends, and it was my favorite time of year. I was just very, very happy. I remember realizing that I had a permanent grin going on, but I couldn't seem to help it. I popped the cork, poured the wine into a few glasses, and threaded my fingers through the stems to deliver them to my guests. When I glanced up, Allison was looking at me from across the room with an expression on her face that I couldn't pinpoint. It was a mixture of sadness, happiness, warmth, and something else I couldn't grasp. I winked at her and continued on to serve my guests. And as I replay the whole thing in my head now, I know what the fourth descriptor was. Without a doubt.

Desire.

I actually gasp out loud. Allison wanted me a year ago.

I immediately begin to second-guess myself. Of course. Could that possibly be what I saw in her face? Am I just that full of myself? It's been a year. Why hasn't she said anything?

Kim.

Duh.

Allison has class. She has integrity. She never would have jeopardized my relationship with Kim. Nor would she have risked our friendship with each other. She hasn't said anything here on vacation because I've been single less than three weeks. I know Allison. I *know* her. She's letting me wallow, grieve, and recover before she says anything. She's sure it's way too soon for me to think about another relationship.

Enter Frankie.

It only occurs to me in this moment that in Frankie, I chose somebody roughly the same size and coloring as Allison. How did I not notice that? Jesus, I'm a dolt. Allison is a lot more feminine than Frankie, but they're the same height, they have the same dark hair, the same piercingly blue eyes, the same magnetism. It's just that Allison uses hers for good, not evil.

I hit the bathroom and try to clean myself up as best I can. My face is puffy. My eyes are red-rimmed. But a splash or two of cold water and the addition of a little makeup go a long way, and in less than half an hour, I'm dressed and somewhat presentable.

I feel like a curtain has been peeled back. But not a heavy curtain…more like a sheer. Something that's kept a blurred layer between me and Allison. And that layer represented our significant others. It's the only thing that makes sense. Now I'm single, and she's single, and maybe it's time we sat down and talked about a few things.

I give myself the once over in the full-length mirror. The light khaki-colored capris I've chosen really accentuate my new tan (I hadn't realized how much color I've actually gotten…a color other than pink). The black short-sleeve Henley is one of my favorites because of the cut…it's slim on my torso and hugs my chest just enough to draw the eye (or so Kim told me once). My hair is loose and lighter because of the sun. I examine my entire form and for the first time, wonder what Allison would think. I slip into my black sandals, pop my phone and key card into my little cross-body bag, and with a big, fortifying breath, I close the door behind me and head to the elevators.

I actually step into one of the cars before the glitch in my plan becomes glaringly obvious to me: I have no earthly idea where Jules's room is.

"Crap."

In the lobby, I wander to the fountain and take a seat, try to regroup. I'm still sure Allison is with Jules and her gang, so I decide to meander around and look for them. Not the most detailed plan known to man, given the sheer size and scope of this place, but it worked when I was looking for Frankie, so I have no reason to think it couldn't work again. I shoot a quick text off to Allison asking where she is, but I get no immediate response.

It's busy here again, more festive. There must be speakers in the ceiling because I can detect the faintest version of *Baby, It's Cold Outside* emanating from somewhere. The Christmas song makes me think of the Christmas movie *Elf* and the scene where Will Ferrell and Zooey Deschanel sing the duet in the ladies' room. Allison and I have watched *Elf* together for the past three Christmases in a row, and the thought of not doing that this year sends me into a sudden spiral of panic, shame, and desperation.

I have to find Allison.

I start with the restaurants. It's lunchtime, so maybe Jules, Jess, Amy, and Allison are eating. It takes me nearly forty minutes to hit each of them, but no sign of my prey.

Next is the pool. The weather is alarmingly similar to the past three days, and instead of making me feel warm and tropical, I feel like I live under a dome and in a scientific experiment to see how quickly people get bored with the same weather over and over and over. Florida is weird.

The same atmosphere permeates the air here as it did in the lobby. There are more people, and they seem happier. The bartenders are busily shuffling around, whirling up tropical drinks in blenders and handing plastic glasses to their poolside servers. I watch as one of them pours a frothy red drink from the blender into a martini glass and garnishes it with a tiny candy cane. I look back at the pool filled with bathing suited people of all sizes and shapes, accented with a backdrop of deep blue sky and glowing sunshine, and I suddenly miss snow so badly it's like a physical ache in my chest.

No sign of Jules or her crew. No sighting of Allison sitting on a lounge chair while a line of women waits to talk to her. Nothing. A check of my phone reveals that Allison has still not responded to my text. I send another.

I sigh, depressed, and head back inside.

I wander and meander and stroll and roam, and I find nothing. No sign of any of them. I'm sure by the time I return to the lobby fountain that I've put close to five miles on my sandals. My feet hurt. I have a blister forming on the inside of my arch. I take a seat at the fountain—the exact same spot I sat over an hour before—and I blow out a frustrated breath. I'm exhausted. I'm beyond exhausted. I've been here for less than four days total, yet it feels like I've been away from my home, away from my *life*, for years. I'm depressed. I'm exasperated. I feel as though the universe has been playing tricks on me. The gods are apparently still getting their kicks with the Mackenzie Campbell action figure, but I know I'm sick to death of always being in the wrong place at the wrong time.

My phone still devoid of any messages from Allison, I lean my head back against the hard marble side of the fountain, close my eyes, and try my best not to dwell on the drastic changes my life has gone through over the past three weeks. It is an utter, indescribable mess, and now I'm stuck fifteen hundred miles from home, alone, at Christmas time, in a state I'm beginning to hate due to all it represents for me. It takes all the energy I have left to keep from bursting into tears of defeat.

"Hey, you."

The voice startles me so much that I literally jump in my seat and clamp a hand to my chest. "Jesus Christ," I mutter to Amy as I try to keep my heart from beating right out of my body.

Amy's smile is friendly and apologetic. "Sorry." She lays a warm hand on my shoulder. "I just saw you and scooted over here. I didn't mean to scare you. What are you doing? Just hanging out?"

I breathe deeply, calming my racing pulse, and tell her, "I've been looking everywhere for you guys." I'm not sure if I successfully hid the accusation in my tone.

"Oh, we went parasailing again. It costs way too much money, but it's so much fun. I didn't want to come down."

"You just got back?" At Amy's nod, I ask, "Was Allison with you? I've been trying to find her, but I've had no luck, and she's not answering my texts."

Amy opens her mouth to speak, closes it, presses her lips together, and just looks at me for a moment, as if rethinking her words. Then she opens her mouth again and speaks slowly. "Kenzie, Allison left for the airport a couple hours ago."

I blink at her, feeling for a split second like she's speaking a language I cannot comprehend. "What?"

"Yeah. I thought you knew. She stopped by our suite last night with her bags and asked if she could crash on the extra bed in Jules's room. This morning, we exchanged e-mail addresses and said our goodbyes because she was grabbing the shuttle to the airport. She didn't tell you that?"

I try to swallow down the lump in my throat, but it won't go down all the way. It just sits there like a hardboiled egg. I shake my head from side to side and am mortified to feel my eyes brimming with tears.

"Oh, sweetie, I'm sorry I just blurted it out like that." Amy leans forward to catch my eyes. "Are you okay?"

I gaze straight ahead, seeing the front desk, but not really *seeing* it, as my vision is blurred, and I'm pretty sure I can feel my heart cracking open in my chest. I blew it this time. I really blew it. I continue to stare as Amy rubs a warm hand up and down my back and new guests spill through the front doors with their luggage.

With their luggage.

They have luggage.

Which can only mean the shuttle is out front.

It's ridiculous to think I can catch her. She's probably halfway home by now. But I have to try. I have no other recourse. This is it. It's my last hurrah.

I jump up from my seat so quickly my shoulder cracks Amy in the jaw. "I'm so sorry," I say, and kiss her on the temple. "I've got to go." And with that, I sprint across the lobby, dodging other guests and their bags like a contestant on a game show running through an obstacle course.

The shuttle is just closing its back doors on the luggage of its passengers. I hit only one step as I jump onboard.

I need to get to the airport.

I have no idea what I'll do if I don't find Allison.

Also, I have no idea what I'll do if I *do* find her.

All I know is that in every romantic movie I've ever seen that has a scene where somebody is trying to catch somebody else at an airport, there is always a happy ending. I'm hoping this is mine.

The shuttle driver is messing with me. I'm sure of it. It feels like I've been riding this damn bus for the better part of my entire existence. It's not The Rainbow's Edge shuttle we took on our way over. I missed that one. This is a general shuttle that hits all the hotels in the area before getting to the airport. I'm pretty sure we've made fifteen stops since I boarded.

"How much longer?" I ask him for the third time.

According to his name tag, he is Juan. Juan's annoyed eyes catch mine in his visor mirror. "Three minutes less than last time you ask," he says in broken English.

I'm sitting in the seat directly behind his driver's seat. It's the seat normally reserved for the most obnoxious passengers, the ones who think the driver has some innate desire to be talked to incessantly for the entire shuttle ride. I hate those people. Today, I *am* those people.

Juan makes a hard right and swings the shuttle into the horseshoe-shaped driveway entrance of a Holiday Inn. I clamp my lips shut before the words, "Oh my *god*, another stop? Are you *freaking kidding me*?!" escape from between them. At this rate, Allison could have flown home and back four times. I'm starting to think maybe this is a stupid idea. I mean, if we were meant to be together, wouldn't it have happened by now? In some way? I don't know. I can't even think. My head is so full, and my brain is so tired of going around and around and around trying to figure it all out, I just want to crawl into bed and sleep for days. Weeks, maybe.

I flop backwards against the seat and sigh. Juan helps a woman aboard the shuttle, then scoots around back to toss her baggage into the open compartment there. The shuttle is pretty full at this point, and the woman—who reminds me of my mother for some reason—takes one of the last two open seats left.

Juan hoists himself up the steps, drops into his seat and closes the double doors. Once we're on the road again and the quiet buzz of conversation has begun, he speaks into the mic attached to his dashboard.

"Next stop: airport."

"Thank god," I mutter. His eyes catch mine in the mirror.

It's another fifteen minutes, but we finally arrive at the airport. At least I think it's the airport. It's not like I can see much around the throngs of people everywhere, though the deafening roar of planes overhead and on the runway is a pretty good sign.

Since I have no bags, I bolt off the shuttle before anybody else and head into the building. It's a zoo. Seriously. There are people everywhere, and I once again curse the beautiful sunny weather for its ability to make me completely forget what time of year it is. Of course the airport is packed. It's three days before Christmas and the last weekend before Christmas. I'm not sure what I was expecting, but it wasn't a mass of people crammed into the place like so many heads of cattle.

Luckily, most people are headed to the desks or to security. I immediately start looking for Allison at the JetBlue counter. That's the airline we used to get here, so I have to assume she'd use them to fly home. I scan the dozens of customers waiting in line. Families, couples, singles, kids, babies, there's something for everybody in that line. Everybody but me. No Allison.

Okay, so maybe she changed airlines. Maybe she had to. Maybe JetBlue was booked and they suggested she try another carrier. I wander slowly down the row of counters, squinting as I scan each line that switches back on itself, people lined up between the ropes like good little soldiers. I don't see her, but there are so many people, I worry it'd be easy to miss her. I force myself to slow down, to search carefully and thoroughly.

Behind me, mounted to the wall, is one of the big screens with arrivals and departures. I move toward that and peruse all the flights. I find three going in our general vicinity, so I start walking to each of the airline counters. In doing so, I pass the line for security, and a wave of sadness washes over me. If Allison's already gone through security, I'll never catch her. I can't get through without a boarding pass.

I pull out my phone. I have three new texts, but none are from her. I send her another one asking where she is, and I think about telling her I'm at the airport, but I don't want to seem too pathetic. I pocket my phone and keep walking, my eyes starting to burn from the search.

The smell of food from a nearby food court is making me drool. Literally, saliva is pooling in my mouth, and I realize that I haven't eaten a thing today. The smell of cinnamon is so teasing, I almost cry because I don't want to take the time to stop and eat. I have to find Allison. The path to the food takes me past a small gift shop and something in the window catches my eye. I decide then and there that it's okay to take the time.

I detour.

Impromptu purchase tucked under my arm, I feel better. More positive. Determined in my quest.

I'm back at the counters. Walking. Scanning. Walking. Scanning.

My positive attitude doesn't last long. I feel like I'm looking for the proverbial needle in a haystack, and it's just not happening. How can I be expected to find one person in this enormous bulk of human bodies? It's an exercise in futility, and when I realize this fact, unanticipated tears spring into my eyes. *Princess Waterworks rides again.* I blew it. I'm never going to find Allison. I'm never going to be able to explain all the things I'm feeling, ask her all the questions I need to ask her. I'll get home, she'll be at her house, she'll continue to ignore my texts. The idea of all of it, all the failure rolled up into one big ball of misery, grabs ahold of my heart and slowly crushes it until the tears have no choice but to clear my lids and roll down my cheeks.

I rifle through my bag and find a tissue to blow my nose. As I do, I see the phone light blink to notify me of a new text. I pull it out as I'm trying to wipe my nose with one hand.

It's from Allison. My heart thuds as I read it.

Don't cry.

Wait. What? My head snaps up, and I scan the lines again, looking at each person slowly and carefully. I don't see her. She obviously sees me, but I don't see her. Where is she? Just as I'm getting frustrated, a thought occurs to me.

I turn around and look *away* from the counters. Behind me.

Allison is sitting on a bench, her bag next to her feet, her legs casually crossed, and detritus from what looks like it might have been her lunch on the space next to her. She gives me a half grin.

I have never been so happy to see somebody in my life, and I don't hesitate. I cross right over to her and wrap my arms around her neck. She hugs me back, which makes me squeeze her tighter. After a long moment, I let go, move her food litter, and sit next to her.

"I have been looking all over this place for you." I try not to sound scolding, but I don't know if I'm entirely successful.

"I know. I've been watching."

I squint at her. "What?"

"You walked past me six times. You kept looking in the same direction." She points at the counters. "That one. I wanted to see how long it would take for you to look in a different one, to think out of the box. You failed. Miserably."

I can't help but laugh. "Add it to my long list of failures this week. How long have you been sitting here?"

"I saw you come in."

I give her a look. Yes, I'm annoyed, but it doesn't matter. I found her. I found Allison. My relief overshadows everything else.

"I really was going to wait, but then you were standing there looking like a lost little girl with your tear-filled eyes, and I couldn't play anymore. I had to let you off the hook." She lifts a hand, waves it like a kid in class wanting to answer a question. "I'm right here."

"Thank god," I say. And I mean it. I hug her again. "I thought you'd left," I say as I pull back and hold her gaze. "I worried you'd left."

"I thought about it," she says, but her eyes don't leave mine. "I wanted to. Unfortunately, it's three days before Christmas. The woman at the counter almost laughed in my face when I asked to change my ticket. She politely controlled herself, I'm happy to say."

"So, you couldn't change your flight?"

"Nope."

"What were you going to do? Just sit here?"

"For a while. I was thinking." Allison gives a sheepish grin.

"And how long have you been sitting here? Thinking?"

Allison glances at her watch. "About four hours."

I chuckle and shake my head. "Well," I say and look her in the eye. "I'm glad you didn't leave."

"Yeah?"

"Yeah."

"How come?"

"Because I want to talk to you."

"About what?"

I give her another look. Her *I'm a smartass* expression fades after a second or two. Then she nods once, giving me her approval to proceed. Of course, now that I have the floor, I'm not sure what to say. I didn't rehearse, which was shortsighted of me I now realize. There was no practice run. I look up at the airport ceiling, follow the beams with my eyes. When I look back down, Allison's blue eyes are fixed on me, expectant but hesitant at the same time, and it occurs to me that part of her is bracing for me to hurt her. Again.

I clear my throat. "I've been kind of stupid," I begin. "Kind of stupid, a little blind." I stop, wet my lips. God, what if my mother is wrong? What if I lay this all out for Allison and she laughs at me? What if she's shocked and horrified? What if she's never actually thought of me like that? I know I'm just panicking. I've gone over this in my head at least a little. There have been looks. There have been glances. And there was Friday night.

"Kim left me."

"Kim's an idiot."

"She doesn't love me."

"Doesn't matter. I love you."

"You do?"

"I always have."

Something else occurs to me then, and I decide to change my tack. I wet my lips. "If I ask you a question, will you answer me honestly?"

"I've never lied to you, Kenzie. Not once."

I nod. "Okay." I take a deep breath. Here goes nothing. "Why did you break up with Marianne? The real truth this time. None of your 'it wasn't working out' blanket vague answer. The *real* truth. Please. Why did you leave Marianne?"

For a split second, Allison has the look of a deer caught in headlights, but to her credit, that passes quickly as her expression changes to one of defeated resignation. She studies her hands while I study her face. I can see her processing something in her head, something she hasn't wanted me to know. When she looks back up at me, though, she's completely open.

"I was in love with somebody else."

"Who?" I ask without missing a beat.

She doesn't break eye contact. "I think you know."

"Please, Allison. I need you to tell me."

And suddenly, her eyes are wet, and she looks away. Those beautiful gorgeously blue eyes well up with tears, something that doesn't happen often with Allison. I want nothing more than to make those tears disappear. I close my hands over hers. "Tell me."

Her voice is no more than a ragged whisper when she speaks. "I've been in love with you since the day we met, Mackenzie." She shakes her head slowly from side to side. "I tried not to be. I really did. I fought it. I fought hard. But I can't help it."

"I don't want you to help it," I tell her and bring my hand up to lay it on her cheek. She presses her face against my palm, closes her eyes for a moment, then looks at me again, this time with concern.

"This is bad timing for you, Kenz," she says. "You can't deal with this right now. Not after what you've been through."

My heart fills to bursting as I look at her, listen to her words that are all about taking care of me, and I know this is where I want to be. Sitting right next to Allison. It's where I'm *supposed* to be, a fact that is suddenly, blindingly clear. "On the contrary, I think this is perfect timing. I think the situation I've been in has helped me to see some things much clearer than before. I think we *finally* got the timing exactly right."

She cocks her head, puzzled.

"Think about it, Allie. When we met and I was single, you were with Marianne. Then I hooked up with Kim, and you and Marianne broke up. Neither of us was ever in the right place to address *us*. But now, we're both here, and we're both available…" I let my voice trail off.

"Have you..." Allison clears her throat, tries again. "Have you...thought of me like that?" Her tone is so tentative, so cautious, that I want to hug her.

"God, yes," I admit, and it's the truth. In that moment, I recall all the times I'd wondered what it would be like to be with Allison, as a partner...as a lover. I'd always quickly shook those thoughts away, put them in a box and shoved them into a corner, as either she or I was unavailable. But now, I open my mind, open that box, and let them come rushing back in. Allison in her Wonder Woman Halloween costume two years ago, with those shapely legs that went on for days. Allison picking me up to take me to a baseball game last summer, top down on her convertible, sunglasses on her face, looking impossibly sexy. Allison ready to impress a potential client, all decked out in her navy blue business suit, heels, and just enough cleavage to warrant a longer peek than normal. And Allison's face when she finally talked me out of the bathroom after Kim dropped her bomb, the expression of satisfaction, but also the desire to hold me until I felt better, which she did.

At my answer, Allison's face is the epitome of relief mixed with a little disbelief, and she turns her hands palms-up so she can grip mine, but I pull mine away. "Wait. I have something for you." I find the little package from the gift store, pull the item out and hand it to her.

Her smile is radiant as she takes the little snow globe from my hand. It's only a couple of inches high with a brown plastic base. Inside the globe is a palm tree and hanging from the palm tree is a red heart ornament. "This is so adorably cheesy."

"Isn't it? I couldn't resist." My voice softens. "It made me think of you."

She shakes the globe, its tiny little snowflakes creating a sparkling white mist around the tree. When she looks at me, her eyes are gleaming. "Thank you. I love it." She shakes it again. "Can you feel it?"

I grin. "The Christmas magic?"

"The Christmas magic."

"Yeah. I think I can." I smile as she shakes it again, and her face has the glow of a child in awe. I want to hug her. I want to wrap my arms around her, feel her arms around me. I want to kiss her. Badly. She looks around us then, as if suddenly noticing the throngs of people. Her eyes come back to mine, and I lay my hand on her thigh, pretty sure we're thinking the same thing. "Come back to the hotel with me."

I don't have to ask her twice. She stands up immediately, pulls up the handle on her bag, and we head for the door, dropping her food litter into the garbage can on our way out.

Chapter Nineteen

THE SHUTTLE RIDE BACK to the hotel is a bit surreal. It's like a replay of our ride on Wednesday, except the circumstances are completely different. I feel like I'm getting a do-over.

We're sitting very close. Allison is wearing jeans, which are too warm for the weather here, but I'm sure she was anticipating the cold at home. I can feel the heat from her thigh as it rests against the much lighter fabric of my capris. We're quiet, and I can't speak for her, but I am enjoying this closeness immensely. I try to be subtle about moving in tighter. She turns to me, and gives me a smile that is so goddamn sexy I literally feel weak in my knees and am suddenly grateful I'm not standing.

Allison turns her gaze to the windows as we pass a strip mall adorned with Christmas lights and silver strings of garland. They seem so out of place given the sunshine and eighty degree weather. Allison leans close to me.

"I never thought I'd say this, but I miss snow."

I nod. "Me, too."

"And cold."

"Me, too."

"This never-changing weather is freaking me out a little bit."

I laugh at that, as I've thought the very same thing. "Me, too!"

Dropping her voice to a whisper, she says, "I hate fucking Florida. Let's never come here again."

"Deal." I hold out my hand and we shake on it, but she doesn't let me go. Instead, she tucks my hand into hers and entwines our fingers. Then she lays both our hands against her thigh, and covers them with her other hand as she continues to gaze out the window. There's something surrounding us now, an aura of some kind. Corny, I know, but it's like any and all walls or barriers between Allison and me—anything that was keeping us from recognizing and acting upon our physical attraction—have suddenly evaporated and now there's this buzzing force field of desire that's encapsulated us. Butterflies float around in my stomach, I'm throbbing and wet between my legs, and if there weren't other people on this shuttle, I might just fling myself right into Allison's lap.

I've never felt like I can't wait before.

It's new, and it's weird.

I like it.

Just when I'm about to start getting frustrated, the shuttle pulls into the horseshoe drive of The Rainbow's Edge. We hop off and are halfway to the front door before Allison skids to a halt.

"Shit. My bag."

I wait as she jogs back to the shuttle, grabs her bag, tips the driver, and practically sprints across the parking lot to me. She snags my hand and tugs me through the lobby to the elevator. As usual, the place is mobbed. There are people everywhere, men and women, couples, singles, groups of friends. We get on the elevator car along with about nine others, and I grimace when I see six other buttons lit up with numbers lower than twenty. I look at Allison. She grins and squeezes my hand.

We wait.

One by one, the car stops at each designated floor. People get off. People get on. It feels like forever, but finally—*finally*—we hit the twentieth floor. We exit the elevator, and head down the hall to our room.

Our room.

That's how I'm thinking about it. Again, weird, but I like it.

We get to our door, and I fish through my little bag for the key card. Allison is standing so tightly behind me I can feel her body heat. Her mouth is close to my ear as she whispers one command.

"Hurry."

I fumble slightly, but manage to get the card into the slot the correct way. The green light pops on, and the lock clicks. We shove through like we're one being, and I barely have the door closed behind me before Allison is pushing me against it, her hands cupping my face, her mouth closing hungrily over mine.

Allison is kissing me.

That thought is the only clear one that runs through my head as I kiss her back with all I have, wrapping my arms around her waist and pulling her in closer. And holy crap, do we kiss well together. Her lips are soft, her mouth is hot, and when I feel her tongue against mine, I can't suppress a moan of desire. My head knocks softly against the door, but I barely notice. I just want more of her, and I slide my hands under her shirt and up her bare back, her skin warm and soft under my palms.

She pulls me away from the door and backs me against the wall, then steps back and holds up a finger, silently telling me to wait. Then she grabs the Do Not Disturb sign, hangs it on the outside doorknob, shuts the door again and throws the deadbolt. Then she's back, and her mouth claims mine again, and my conscious thoughts blur as I let myself melt into her.

I know it sounds a little corny, but I've never felt like this before. Who says that at thirty-five years old? But it's true. I've never felt like this. Not with Kim. Certainly not with Kim. Not with any of my previous lovers (and there haven't really been all that many). I've never felt such urgency, such flat-out desire for somebody. More than that, the thing that really has me amazed, is that it's never, ever felt so incredibly right. So perfect. It's like

Allison's hands were made for my body as her palms slide up the sides of my rib cage, under my shirt. Her thumbs graze across my nipples, and even over the fabric of my bra, it pulls a cry from me as I feel them stand at attention for her. And even more than that, I want her. I *want* her. I can't remember ever wanting somebody so badly before. I push forward, propelling Allison backwards until her legs hit the side of the bed and she sits. I keep pushing and in seconds, she's on her back on the bed, me laying atop her, our mouths still fused, our tongues still pushing against one another's. I slide my hand up under her top, feel the heat from her skin, the softness of her belly, the pleasing roundness of her breasts. This time, it's her turn to moan into my mouth.

I raise up so I can help her pull her shirt over her head, and she takes advantage by flipping our positions. Now she's above me, but I count getting her top off as a small victory for me because my eyes feast on her bare torso, her skin bronzed, her bra simple and white and dazzlingly sexy. Her eyes are a bit hazy with desire, her hair a little messy, falling across her forehead, and I decide immediately that it's a look I like on her: tousled and flushed.

"You're so beautiful," I say to her softly as I run my fingertips along the side of her breast.

"Hey, that's my line," she replies. "And stop distracting me." She playfully slaps my hand away, then descends on my mouth again.

There's something incredibly sensual about a really good kiss. Not to take away from the joys of actual sex, because those are amazing, obviously. But in my opinion, a *really* good kiss sets the stage for everything that follows. It's like the opening act. If it's not good, you're not as excited for what comes next. And if it's really good, you can let it go on and on and on. That's how Allison kisses me. I want what comes next, yes. But I don't want to stop kissing her. It's erotic, and it's carnal, and I just want more.

Allison is kneeling above me, a knee on either side of my hips. Suddenly, she sits up, reaches down for the front of my shirt, and pulls me to a sitting position with it. Her eyes never leaving mine, she grabs the hem of my shirt and yanks it up, over my head, and off, leaving me in my black bra and capris. Her eyes skim over my skin and I swear to god, I can feel them. Then she takes my face in her hands and kisses me deeply. I grab her torso and hold on for dear life.

I don't notice she's unclasped my bra until she's pulling it off me, and I have to shift my arms to help. Her lips travel down my neck, across my collar bone, and with a gentle nudge, I'm on my back again just before her mouth closes over my nipple. Some primal sound is forced from my lungs as she lavishes attention on my breasts, first one, then the other, then back again. My hands are in her hair, grasping her head, my thoughts a bit convoluted as aching pleasure pushes everything else out of my brain.

I have no idea how much time has passed. I don't care. I'm delirious with desire, as if nobody has ever known what to do to my breasts but Allison. It's crazy. I'm actually woozy. It occurs to me that she's still in her bra and her jeans. I reach around her for the clasp, which I can't quite get to. Allison shifts from my breasts back to my mouth, and I lose all focus. She grabs my wrist, then takes the other, and pins them above my head with one hand. I put up a feeble struggle, and when she pulls back to look at me, I can see by the spark in her eyes that she likes it. I do it again, but of course, I don't really want to get away. I would be perfectly happy to be held prisoner by Allison forever. She arches one sexy eyebrow at my lame attempt to free myself, then lowers her mouth to my nipple, her eyes never leaving mine as she bites down on it, not hard, but enough to get my attention, enough to force a little cry from my lips.

Jesus Christ, I'm pretty sure I'm going to just explode into flames.

Still holding my gaze—and my hands—Allison comes back up so we're face to face. She kisses me again, and as her tongue pushes into my mouth, I feel her fingers working at the button on my capris. She flips it open with little effort and slides the zipper down, kissing me all the while. When her fingers slip under the waistband of my panties and into what must be massive amounts of wetness she's created, my entire body arches up into hers, my arms still pinned, my loud groan filling the room. She's pushed me so high that it only takes a few strokes from her very adept fingers before I reach orgasm, loudly calling her name, riding it out as long as I can even as I feel her watching my face.

It seems like forever before my muscles finally relax and my body settles back down onto the bed. When I open my eyes, Allison is gazing down at me, the smile on her face equal parts satisfaction and love. She lets my wrists go, and I immediately reach up to stroke her face. My breaths are still coming in ragged pants, but I say what's in my heart. I don't want to wait.

"I love you," I tell her.

"It took you long enough to figure it out," she says, the softness of her voice taking out any sting. "I love you, too."

The element of surprise is mine as I expertly flip her onto her back. The shocked expression on her face makes me laugh, but only for a moment. Then I give her my best smoldering look and say, "My turn." Her swallow is audible, and I waste no time pushing her bra up over her breasts and descending upon them with my mouth. A small cry emanates from her, and I'm hit with a wave of power and satisfaction. I want this woman. Oh, how I want this woman. I want to touch her and taste her and pull sounds from her she didn't know she could make.

The jeans are a hindrance, and I tell her so as I unfasten the fly and pull them off from the ankles. She laughs as I do, and when I look at her, I'm hit with such a wave of joy and love that it closes up my throat. I stop to meet her eyes, and I swallow hard. Her expression softens, and she smiles.

"Come here," she says.

I toss her jeans to the floor, shuck my own remaining clothing, and go to her, lying on top of her, both of us completely naked, and kiss her with all the strength I can muster. When I pull back, I tell her I love her for the second time.

Her body is stunning. I'm not surprised by this fact. I've suspected it for a long time. But to actually see her here, lying prone beneath me, her skin waiting for my hands, her center glistening for me, I'm struck by her beauty. There's nothing about her that stands out by itself; she's fairly average in size. Her breasts are not large and not small. Her hips are nicely rounded. Her skin is smooth and soft. But all of it together makes her nothing short of magnificent. I want to touch every single inch of her.

I try not to rush. There's plenty of time, but suddenly kissing her mouth is not enough. I skim my lips down her neck, stop on the pulse point there, feel her heartbeat against my tongue. I continue down her body, stopping at each breast for a few minutes before moving further south, and I'm happily aware of her near-panting as I detour around her belly button, tease it with my tongue.

I feel her hands tighten in my hair. "Mackenzie," she hisses. "Please. You're killing me."

I smile against her belly and decide it's time for relief. She lets me position her legs so I can fit my shoulders between them. The mixture of the heat and the scent of her arousal coming from the apex of her thighs is like a drug that intoxicates me, and I inhale deeply before lowering my mouth to her.

She cries out my name, and I smile as I work, exploring the folds of skin, testing and teasing to see what she likes and what she doesn't. She's soaked, which fills me with a wicked sense of pride, and I realize that I'm going to have to test and explore later because, like me, she is far too aroused to last long. Within a few short moments, her hips come up off the bed, and I hold tightly to them so I don't lose my place. She whimpers my name this time, and her grip tightens on my head; I take that as a cue not to move, so I stay completely still and feel her center throb against my tongue. I can't remember ever being happier.

A beat goes by. Another. Then her grip loosens, and her hips slowly lower, and I gently remove my mouth, causing her to spasm slightly. I rest my head against the warmth of her bare thigh and give her a moment to catch her breath.

"Come here," she commands me for the second time, and I do as I'm told. When our bodies are even, I see that her eyes are glassy.

"Allie, are you okay?" I ask, worried. "Did I hurt you?"

She smiles through her tears and shakes her head. "No. You didn't hurt me. You did the opposite."

I catch a tear with my fingertip. "Why are you crying?"

She reaches up, tucks some of my hair behind my ear. "I just never thought we'd get here. I never thought I'd be able to...have you like this. Or have you have *me* like this. They're happy tears, believe me."

"Well, for what it's worth, I plan on *having* you many, many, *many* more times. Just so you know."

"Consider me warned," she says, then turns herself toward me so I'm on my back. Before I can utter another word, her mouth closes over mine. She kisses me senseless before telling me, "I am *so* not done with you yet."

It's well into the evening before we give each other a break. I have seriously never enjoyed sex so much, never *not* wanted to stop at some point. Allison and I are made for each other...at least our bodies are. I am sore and dehydrated, and one look at her naked body returning from the bathroom with two glasses of water makes me want her all over again.

"Get that predatory look out of your eye, young lady," she says with playful scolding as she hands me a glass. "I need to catch my breath. You're exhausting." With a wink, she adds, "In a totally good way, of course."

"Of course," I reply and drink down the entire glass of water in about four swallows.

"Are you hungry?"

I nod, only realizing it as she asks. I'm famished.

"Room service?"

A grin splits my face. "Naked eating? Fabulous idea."

We call and order, and when the knock on the door comes, Allison decides to be the one to "take one for the team" as she calls it, and she puts on boxers and a T-shirt while I shut my naked self in the bathroom. I listen to her direct the waiter where to put our food. They make small talk. When the door clicks shut, I pop back out and look at the spread we ordered. My stomach growls loudly and we both laugh.

"Yeah, I'm hungry. I haven't eaten since…have I eaten today? I think I got up and immediately started looking for you. Holy crap, no wonder I'm starving." I swipe a dinner roll off the tray and take an enormous bite. It's warm and tastes heavenly.

"You had eye sex with the cinnamon bun booth at the airport," Allison reminds me.

"Oh, my god, I was starving. Notice I didn't stop to eat. Finding you was more important."

"I noticed," she says, then reaches to wipe a crumb from the corner of my mouth.

I take a playful swat at her, then move my finger up and down in an all-encompassing gesture at her. "Naked eating means naked. Off."

She obeys by stripping off the T-shirt, and I stop chewing as she does so. My god, she's beautiful. How did I not notice before? How did I manage to program myself to not see her? She slides the boxers down her legs, seemingly unaware of my ogling. 'Seemingly' is the operative word because without looking at me, she says, "Stop it." Then lifts the lids off the food to see what we've got.

"Stop what?" I ask with feigned innocence.

"Staring at me like that. We need to eat or we're both going to drop." She winks at me, and I feel that sexual pang in the pit of my stomach again. Jesus, one afternoon in bed with Allison has turned me into a nymphomaniac.

The food is wonderful. I've come to expect nothing less from this place. We each ordered cheeseburgers with the works, except for onions, and they're thick and juicy. The fries are hot and salty, just the way I like them. We sit on the bed, lights off, balcony window open to the breeze, and enjoy our first dinner together since…

Since what? I wonder. Since having sex? That's the most accurate. I almost thought "since we've been a couple," but is that the case? Are we a couple?

"So what comes next?" Allison asks, and I marvel over how often she seems to be in my head.

"Well, we can watch TV, have more sex, feed each other the chocolate mousse. Not necessarily in that order. There's also a hot tub that we've very sadly neglected to use thus far in our trip." I wink at her.

"Ha ha. That's not what I mean and you know it. Not that we won't be in that tub before the night is through." She pops a French fry into her mouth and waits for me as she chews. When I don't answer right away, she moves over to the desk where the bottle of champagne we ordered chills in an ice bucket. "I'm opening this." I'm not sure if she's telling me or herself, but I watch as she expertly pops the cork.

"I have to say, there aren't a lot of things in my memory that are sexier than you opening a bottle of champagne with no clothes on."

Her grin is adorable as she fills two flutes, the cleft in her chin very prominent. Handing me my glass, she folds one leg up underneath her butt and sits. "This has been the most amazing afternoon of my life, Mackenzie," she says quietly, holding up her glass for a toast. "No pressure. I just want to know what you're thinking."

"Agreed on the amazing," I say and touch my glass to hers. The delicate ping is a pretty little sound, and we both smile as we sip. I have so much in my head, so many things rolling around, and I'm not sure what to say and what to keep to myself, what's real and what's paranoia.

"Okay. I'll go." Allison studies the bubbles in her champagne for a long moment before she speaks again. "As I said, this will go down in the history books as the best afternoon of my life." Her tongue darts out to wet her lips. "I'm not stupid, and I am not unrealistic. You've been single for about three weeks. I don't expect you to jump into anything deep with me." She takes a deep breath, has trouble meeting my eyes. "That being said, I hope that you'll think about giving us a shot. Just think about it. I think we've already proven just how good together we are."

I adore her. I realize it fully in that moment. I love her. I do. And I'm scared. "God there are so many factors here, aren't there? So many what-ifs?" Allison nods, watching me. I decide now isn't the time to hold back. If anything, it's the time to lay it all out. All of it. Cards on the table. There's no other way. "I'd be married to her right now if Kim hadn't left me." Allison's eyes twinkle, and I know what's next and join in.

"That bitch," we both say, then grin at one another. I swallow, look down at the food, then look back up and say it again. "I'd be married right now."

"I know."

"Would we still be friends?" The thought only occurs to me right then. If Allison has been in love with me for years, what would she have done when I married somebody else?

"I was actually looking at apartments in Madison." She picks at an invisible spot on the comforter.

"Madison? As in *Wisconsin*? *That* Madison?" At her nod, I'm not sure what to say. "Wow," is all I can manage.

"Yeah. I just didn't know if I could watch you start a life with somebody else." She clears her throat, and when she looks up at me, her eyes shimmer. "I always thought I'd be fine, but the past six or eight months have been hard. I don't know why. I mean, when you hooked up with Kim, I moved you squarely into the 'friend' category. I knew I didn't have a chance. And I was okay with that. I just wanted you to be happy. But then…"

Her voice trails off, and I pick up for her because I start to get it. "You didn't like Kim."

"She wasn't good to you," Allison says, and her tone is hard. "She was selfish. If she'd treated you better, I think I'd have been okay. I wouldn't have liked it, but I could have gotten past it if you were happy. If she'd treated you like I would have treated you, I could accept that."

"But she didn't."

"Not even close."

I smile at her. I can't help it. My heart is filled with warmth, and I reach out and stroke her face, but pull back when something else occurs to me. "If I hadn't gotten blasted by those damn rum runners, I would have slept with Frankie. You know that, right?"

Allison nods again, slowly. "I do know that. God, I hated that bitch. The second you told me about the closed circuit cameras, I hated her. What a snake." Then with a snort, she adds, "She's not even your type. *You* know *that*, right?"

I laugh. I can't help it because Allison is right on the money. "I know! What the hell? And by the way, Jules is not your type either."

At that, Allison gives me a look I can't quite read. "I know that. Did you think I was interested in her?"

I narrow my eyes at her. "Weren't you? Sure seemed like you were."

"Wait…you were jealous of Jules?"

It occurs to me to deny it, and I'm about to do so when I realize that I'm being silly. Cards on the table, wasn't that my thinking just moments ago? I clear my throat, swallow, look away, and say softly, "Yes. I was."

When I turn back to Allison, she's got an expression on her face that's a weird combination of satisfaction and love. And then suddenly, we're both laughing. Hard. To the point where tears begin to flow. It takes a while, but once we calm down, Allison's face grows serious.

"You know me, Kenz, probably better than anybody. I don't really believe in stuff like Fate or Destiny or a higher power." She stops to swallow. I hear it. "But I have to believe that all of this stuff happened for a reason…that we were *supposed* to end up right here, right now, just like this."

"In a hotel room eating cheeseburgers naked?"

"Yes. That. Exactly that. How else does any of this make any sense at all?"

"It doesn't."

"Right?"

I get up, take her glass and mine to the desk. Then I clear the tray of food off the bed, take the two small bowls of chocolate mousse and hand them to her, refill our glasses. We move to the head of the bed so we're leaning back against the headboard, scoot our legs under the covers, and eat our dessert together.

"I know it's probably not smart for us to jump right into something," Allison says. "I get that. I do. But maybe we could go slow, take our time, see what happens. You know?"

I look at her, and I can't describe all the things I feel inside. Love, desire, gratitude, protectiveness—and I realize in a lightning bolt of a moment that those are all things you should feel for your partner, your spouse, the person you want to spend your life with, and I can't explain it other than to say my entire being relaxes, like —just as Allison said—I'm exactly where I'm supposed to be. "I think that's a great idea, Allie." And I have never meant anything more.

She blinks those clear blue eyes at me, almost like she's not sure she heard me correctly. "You do?"

"I do. And you know who else thinks it's a great idea?"

Allison furrows her brows, and moves to take a sip of champagne. "Who?"

"My mother."

Champagne sprays across the bed. "What?"

I'm laughing now, both at the expression on Allison's face and at the alarming idea that my mother was right about my love life. I give Allison a brief synopsis of my earlier conversation with Mom and end by saying, "So, yeah. My mother would have chosen you over Kim any day of the week."

"I have always liked your mother. She's a smart woman."

"Apparently, the feeling is mutual."

We sip our drinks in companionable silence for a long moment. Allison reaches out to her nightstand and closes her hand around the little snow globe. "I love this, by the way," she tells me as she gives it a shake and watches the snow float around the palm tree.

"I saw it and immediately thought of you. I had to have it."

"You know why I love it? Because it tells me you were listening when I told you the story of my grandmother. I told Marianne that story at least six times, yet she never remembered hearing it."

For a moment, I'm sad for Allison, sad for the time she spent with somebody who didn't love her the way she should be loved. How do we end up with people who are not good matches for us? It happens all the time. I imagine it's more common to end up with the wrong person than the right one. How is it that people choose so poorly so often? And when we don't choose poorly—

when we make the *exact right choice*—how is it decided who gets lucky? What made Kim leave me and my night with Frankie an epic fail so that I'd end up here with Allison discussing the future and our feelings for each other—feelings that have been here all along for both of us, but that we tucked away in dark corners of our minds and our hearts? I don't understand any of it, and trying to makes my brain hurt. Instead, I put my empty dessert bowl on the night stand, reach for the remote and click on the television as I sip champagne. My thumb hits the channel select button exactly three times before Will Ferrell dressed in a green elf costume fills the screen. *Elf* is on. I can hardly believe it.

Allison and I look at each other, then burst into laughter.

"Well, if that's not the icing on the cake of a perfect evening," she says, and lifts her arm to make room for me. "Come over here."

I scoot closer and tuck myself against her warm skin as we slink down under the covers, my head on Allison's shoulder, her arm around me in loving protection, and we settle in as Buddy the Elf leads his listeners through the field of swirly-twirly gumdrops in his tale of finding love at Christmas. I notice Allison still has the little snow globe I bought her held tightly in her hand. I squeeze my arm around her waist, place a gentle kiss on her shoulder.

"Merry Christmas, Allison," I whisper. "I love you."

"I love you, too." I feel her warm lips on my forehead. "Merry Christmas, sweetheart."

THE END

By Georgia Beers

Novels

Finding Home
Mine
Fresh Tracks
Too Close to Touch
Thy Neighbor's Wife
Turning the Page
Starting From Scratch
96 Hours
Slices of Life
Snow Globe

Anthologies

Outsiders

Georgia Beers
www.georgiabeers.com